PIE RATS

THE ISLAND OF DESTINY

Cyclone Sea

Western Passage

DRUMSTICK ISLAND

THE CRESCENT SEA

PHOENIX ISLAND

Devil's Cliffs

SEA SHANTY ISLAND

RUINED CITADEL

King River

West

Silver Falls

Eastern River

ISLAND OF KINGS

Southern Passage

QUEEN ISLAND

CLAW'S REACH

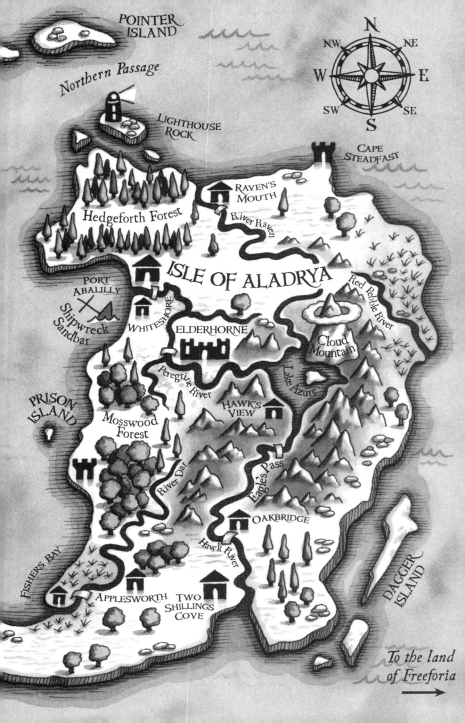

PIE RATS

THE ISLAND OF DESTINY

CAMERON STELZER

Illustrations by the Author

DAYDREAM
PRESS

For my sister, Alison, the nurturer.
Guiding hands shape precious destinies.

First published by Daydream Press, Brisbane, Australia, 2014
Text and illustrations copyright © Dr Cameron Stelzer 2014
Illustrations are watercolour and pen on paper

National Library of Australia Cataloguing-in-Publication Entry
Author: Stelzer, Cameron, 1977 –
Title: The Island of Destiny / by Cameron Stelzer
ISBN: 978 0 9874615 2 0 (pbk.)
Series: Stelzer, Cameron, 1977 – Pie Rats; bk. 3
Target audience: For primary school age.
Subjects: Rats – Juvenile fiction. Pirates – Juvenile fiction.
Dewey number: A823.4

Printed in China by Everbest Printing Co Ltd

Loyalty before all else, even pies.
The Pie Rat Code

The Cyclone Sea

The afternoon sky was a grey blur of clouds and rain. An icy wind howled from the east. The ocean frothed and foamed.

A small, two-masted ship ploughed through the crashing waves. Her course was straight. Her sails were full. The black-furred rat behind the wheel adjusted his soggy eye patch and checked the compass.

'North-north-west,' he muttered in a deep, commanding voice. 'We're still on course. Where is this island?'

'It can't be far, Captain,' replied the young rat next to him. 'We passed Drumstick Island hours ago.'

Captain Black Rat lowered the compass and sighed. 'I hope you're right, Whisker. The Cyclone Sea is not a forgiving place. If we've overshot our destination, we're in deep water!'

Whisker shuddered. *Deep water!* He felt his tail drop to the deck. Painful memories came rushing back ...

He was sinking into the silent depths, watching helplessly as the little red boat carrying his parents and sister vanished into the terrible cyclone above ...

He tried to block the vision.

You're going to find them, he told himself. *Don't lose hope.*

He touched the edge of his missing right sleeve and stared through the rain at the thundering sky. He was in a storm, not a cyclone.

'The *Apple Pie's* been through worse, Captain,' he said slowly.

The Captain looked grave. 'Not with a hull full of holes, she hasn't. Those rock-throwing Tasmanian devils made a right old mess of the old girl!'

Whisker glanced down at the deck of the *Apple Pie* and winced. Splintered boards and crater-like holes filled his vision, a lasting reminder of the devilish encounter.

A third rat staggered onto the helm, counting every step as he went. '… five, six, seven.' He was no taller than a child, but the battle scars on either cheek gave him an older, roguish appearance. He waved a golden hook through the air in a futile attempt to swat the falling raindrops.

'Hook Hand Horace, reporting for duty, sir!' he announced, clicking his heels.

'Always the showman, aren't you, Horace,' the Captain muttered. 'Anything to report from below?'

'We're not sinking – yet,' Horace replied optimistically. 'Fred's resealing the holes with coagulated pie gravy. It should hold us until we reach the island …'

'What about the creature?' Whisker cut in. 'Rat Bait warned us of a fierce sea creature that guards the Island of Destiny. I doubt gravy will keep it at bay.'

'I don't have a harpoon, if that's what you're asking,' Horace said, draining the rainwater from his oversized, purple hat. 'But I could make you a net – just in case.'

The Captain nodded. 'First rule of thumb, Horace: If you think you'll need it, you'll *definitely* need it!'

Horace gave the Captain a salute with his hook and

descended the slippery stairs. Whisker shook the rain drops from his tail and scurried after him.

'WHISKER! Over here! On the double!'

Whisker heard the command and immediately changed direction. As a Pie Rat apprentice, he was used to being bossed around, especially by the Captain's niece, Ruby.

Whisker dodged three large holes in the deck and skidded along the wooden pastry crust bulwark to where the ship's boatswain stood waiting for him. Even in the soaking rain, Ruby Rat looked like she'd just stepped out of the Portside Boutique. Her crimson eye patch sat neatly over her right eye, her cherry red vest and matching bandanna were crease-free and her two scarlet scissor swords dangled symmetrically off her belt. She stared blankly at Whisker with her emerald green eye.

Ruby, like her uncle, the Captain, had a nasty temper. She could snap at the drop of a hat (or a mis-tied rope, as was often the case). Whisker was never quite sure how he should act around her.

He felt his *over-emotional* tail twitch nervously behind his back and hoped the unruly fur on the top of his head was lying flat for a change. He casually raised his paw to check. Tangled tufts of fur stuck up like the leaves of a pineapple.

'W-what can I help you with, Ruby?' he stammered, suddenly self-conscious.

'I need a paw to adjust the jib sail,' Ruby said, deadpan. 'Horace ties knots like he eats spaghetti – messily!'

Whisker breathed a sigh of relief. Horace was always in trouble for something.

'Sure, Ruby,' he said, relaxing his tail.

He climbed onto the bowsprit, the long silver spoon

ing from the front of the ship. Huge waves crashed over the tail of the Mer-Mouse below, sending water cascading over the sides of her golden pie. Part mouse, part mermaid, the ship's majestic figurehead was always a sight to behold.

Whisker hooked his tail around the spoon and slowly reached for the human-sized pair of red underpants that acted as the jib sail. Without looking, he curved his paw around one of the yellow clothes pegs holding the sail in place. The peg felt strangely warm and soft.

Ruby shot Whisker a strange look. Whisker glanced up, his sky-blue eyes growing wide in panic. He wasn't holding a peg at all. He was clutching Ruby's paw.

'S-sorry,' he gasped, pulling away.

Ruby's expression didn't change. Whisker felt his face flushing.

Say something, he told himself. *Crack a joke. Make her laugh. It always works for Horace …*

'Y-you did ask me for a paw,' he gabbled.

'So I did,' Ruby said, managing a small grin. 'Now lend me another one so I can tighten this rope.'

Trying to act natural, Whisker helped Ruby tension the line supporting the jib sail, keeping his eyes on his paws at all times.

He finished double-checking his knot and looked through the rain to the two masts of the ship: a giant silver knife and a colossal silver fork. The T-shirt mainsail and handkerchief foresail appeared secure in the gusty wind. The cutlery-clothesline combination never ceased to amuse Whisker – especially when he considered they were attached to an enormous pie-shaped hull.

Ruby followed Whisker's gaze across the deck.

'Mouse knots,' she murmured, pointing to the fixing points holding the sails in place. 'Small fingers equal strong knots. Thank goodness for stowaway school mice ...'

She was interrupted by a frantic *BUZZ* from the corner of the deck. Whisker turned to see a large green blowfly, wearing a red and white striped jumper, clutching the edge of a barrel.

'What is it, Smudge?' Ruby asked.

The loyal mascot of the Pie Rats pointed into the storm with one arm and held on tightly with the other five.

'I think he's spotted something,' Whisker said.

'Rain,' Ruby huffed. 'A whole lot of rain.'

Smudge shook his head and pointed again.

Whisker squinted out to sea, hoping to catch a glimpse of a rock or an island. All he could see was rain, more rain and a blurry patch that looked remarkably like rain.

'Find Fred, Whisker!' Ruby snapped. 'He'll tell us if there's anything out there.'

Without protest, Whisker scampered down the stairs in search of the sharpest lookout of the crew, Fish Eye Fred.

The ship lurched from side to side with every passing wave, bouncing Whisker off the walls of the narrow corridor. He heard the sounds of silver plates clanging to the floor and the echo of Pencil Leg Pete's spare pencils rolling around a cabin. Finding the upper level deserted, he made his way to the cargo hold at the bottom of the ship.

Peering through the doorway, Whisker could see orange light radiating from a lantern in the centre of the cluttered room. Horace scrounged through a pile of ropes in the corner, while Pete splashed his red pencil leg in a pool of water, issuing orders to Fish Eye Fred and the three school mice.

THE PIE RATS

(and honorary members of the crew)

Pencil Leg Pete

Captain Black Rat

Smudge

Whisker

Mr Tribble

Fish Eye Fred

Eaton

Ruby Rat

Emmie

Hook Hand Horace

To his right, Whisker noticed a large hole in the side of the hull, boarded up with wooden planks, stamped *FIREWORKS*. Fred was busy painting a brown liquid over the cracks. Emmie and her twin brother Eaton applied the gravy-like substance to small leaks, while Mr Tribble examined the opposite side of the hull for further damage.

Mr Tribble looked up through smeared glasses as Whisker entered the room.

'Hello, Whisker,' he said in his polite teacher's voice. 'Have you come to assist?'

'Err, not exactly,' Whisker said, almost slipping on a fresh patch of gravy. 'I need to borrow Fred. Smudge has spotted something in the rain.'

Pete screwed up his bony white nose and sniffled, 'Can't you see we're all busy?'

'*Some* of us are busy,' Horace muttered. 'Others are just paddling in puddles!'

Pete narrowed his pink albino eyes at Horace. 'Supervising is a very important role, especially for a quartermaster of my calibre!'

Horace gave Pete a dismissive wave of his hook and returned to the ropes.

'I'm sure we can spare Fred for a couple of minutes,' Mr Tribble said diplomatically.

'Alright then!' Pete snapped. 'But you're on gravy duty, Tribble. That stuff gets up my nose!'

Fred handed his saucepan of gravy to Mr Tribble and grunted goodbye to Eaton and Emmie. Eaton looked up and, as usual, said nothing. Emmie, the recently appointed *hygiene officer* of the ship, shook her head.

'You can't go up there looking like that, Uncle Fred,' she

16

said. 'You've got gravy all over your arms!'

Fred removed his white chef's hat from his enormous head and used it to wipe the gravy from his tattooed arms.

'Better?' he asked.

'You've still got a spot on your earring!' Emmie scolded. 'Ruby would be ever so furious if it dripped on her deck.'

Fred gave his safety pin earring a quick wipe and stuck his gravy-stained hat back on his head.

'Now we go,' he grunted.

The giant rat followed Whisker up to the deck, whistling an out-of-tune rendition of *Rain, Rain Go Away* through his protruding front teeth. The rain had eased slightly when they reached the top of the stairs, but the wind was no less fierce.

'Over here!' Ruby hissed from the bow of the ship.

Fred lumbered towards her, swivelling his enormous eye from west to east.

'Lots of rain,' he remarked.

Ruby frowned at Smudge. 'I told you!'

Fred fixed his eye on a point out to sea.

'Black rocks to the east,' he muttered.

'East!' Whisker exclaimed. 'Are you sure?'

Fred nodded. 'Looks like an island.'

Smudge folded four arms across his chest, awaiting an apology. The wind blew him straight off the barrel.

'Land ahoy!' Ruby shouted. 'Starboard side.'

The Captain raised a short telescope to his eye and peered through.

'That's our island!' he declared. 'And to think, we were sailing straight past it.'

There was a cacophony of bumps and thumps as Horace

leapt onto the deck in a tangle of ropes and sinkers.

'Shiver me shipwrecks!' he cried, 'What have I missed?'

'A whole lot of rain ...' Ruby smirked. 'Oh, and Fred found the Island of Destiny.'

Horace gave Fred a friendly prod with his hook. 'Good work, big fella!'

Smudge waved two arms in the air as if to say, *hey what about me? I saw it first!*

The Captain lowered his telescope, swinging the wheel to his right. The *Apple Pie* turned eastward into the wind and an icy blast of rain smacked the crew head on.

'Brrrr,' Horace shivered dramatically.

'Drop the anchor and haul in the sails,' the Captain commanded. 'We can't sail into this headwind, and I won't risk tacking and losing the island.'

Ruby, Whisker and Horace scrambled over to the sails, lowering the enormous items of clothing, while Fred attempted to drop the anchor. There was a loud *CLUNK* as the anchor line came to the end of the spool.

'Oh dear, oh double dear,' Fred groaned. 'We're in deep, deep water.'

Ruby leapt from the mast. 'The anchor hasn't reached the sea floor, Captain. We can't just drift; the wind will blow us miles from the island.'

The Captain was silent, considering his options. Whisker looked east. The rain appeared to be clearing, though he still couldn't see the island with his naked eye.

'We have no choice,' the Captain said, begrudgingly. 'We'll sail short legs to the south-east and then to the north-east to catch the wind. Hopefully we'll reach the island before nightfall. I want Smudge and Fred at the bow of the ship. Let me know the moment you lose sight of the island. Ruby and Horace, you're responsible for the sails. Whisker, you're on the helm with me.'

'Aye aye, Captain,' cheered the crew.

Whisker hurried up the stairs to where the Captain waited anxiously behind the wheel.

'Whisker,' he said in a low voice, 'you remember Rat Bait's story about the island, don't you?'

Whisker nodded slowly, but said nothing. It was a touchy subject, to say the least. The Captain's father, Ratsputin, had once attempted to reach the Island of Destiny – and failed. Following his disastrous voyage, Ratsputin deserted his crew and his family. Whisker knew the Captain harboured a deep resentment towards his father and thought it safer if he kept his mouth shut and let the Captain do the talking.

The Captain continued speaking through gritted teeth, 'My father experienced these exact conditions when he sailed to the island. It was a stormy afternoon. There were sharp rocks, pounding waves …'

'The Treacherous Sea,' Whisker said quietly. 'The *Princess Pie* and her crew barely made it out.'

The Captain stroked his chin thoughtfully. 'If we're going to risk the Sea, we'll need a safe passage. I doubt our hull will hold if we collide with a rock or a sea creature.' He straightened his back. 'My father may have failed, but he was ill-prepared. We know the dangers we face and we have the King's Key – something he never possessed.'

'I can examine the key for clues,' Whisker said, eager to end the conversation. 'Maybe there's something we haven't spotted.'

The Captain nodded. 'This may be our only chance of finding the treasure.'

A treasure with the power to alter one's very destiny,

Whisker recalled. He dared to imagine – *the power to find my family.*

'I'm depending on you, Whisker,' the Captain said soberly. 'We all are.'

TWO

The Rock of Hope

With the weight of the *Apple Pie* on his shoulders, Whisker descended the short flight of stairs to the navigation room.

He found the Forgotten Map and the King's Key lying in the centre of the table. A rough tracing of the map sat nearby, courtesy of Pencil Leg Pete.

Just in case, Whisker thought.

He brushed the wet fringe out of his eyes and placed the King's Key over the hole in the island, completing the map. Glancing down at the riddle, he read: *Dark and Treacherous your voyage may be, keep Hope in your sights as you pass through the Sea.*

Whisker examined the map closely, aware that the misplaced capitals were place names. The Treacherous Sea was a rocky lagoon surrounded by high cliffs. There was one entrance from the ocean and one place to go ashore: a river estuary flowing around the Rock of Hope.

Our destination, he told himself.

The rocks appeared to be concentrated in the centre of the lagoon, forming a deadly obstacle course. Whisker ran his finger to the left and right of the rocks.

Two clear passages, he pondered, *and one sea creature.*

The Island of Destiny
Directly north-north-west of Drumstick Island

My key is not found in the ground.
It moves through air without a sound.
A treasure for a rich king's throne,
its guard appears as leaves and stone.

Dark and Treacherous your voyage may be,
keep Hope in your sights as you pass through the Sea.
Uncover the key and enlighten your mind,
but wisdom is found in the shadows behind.

He explored the map for clues, reading and rereading the riddle, but found no mention of the creature or which direction to sail.

Struggling for clarity, he thought back to the jungle citadel where the Pie Rats first discovered the key. He'd seen directional symbols carved on the palace doorways – *Right passage up … left passage down …* Whisker remembered two symbols in particular: the right paw of royalty and the left paw of despair.

Right leads to riches, Whisker considered. *Maybe we should take the right passage through the lagoon?*

He looked back at the Island of Destiny. The island had its own symbol – two arrows, representing the twin mountains of the island: Mt Mobziw and Mt Moochup.

The left mountain holds the treasure, Whisker thought, *so maybe left, not right, is the correct direction …?* He let his head drop into his paws in frustration.

'There's only one way to resolve this,' he muttered.

He rolled up the map and slid it into a canister, sealing the top with a cork. Wedging the canister into his belt next to his green scissor sword, he picked up the key.

If the map can't give me an answer, he thought, *maybe the island can.*

Whisker had no idea how long he'd been in the navigation room. He staggered onto the windy deck to discover the world outside had changed. The rain had cleared and the sun poked through gaps in the separating clouds. The entire crew was gathered in the centre of the deck, witnessing the spectacle in front of them.

Sharp rocks dotted the ocean ahead, marking the

entrance to the Treacherous Sea. Steep cliffs of basalt rock rose to the north. Sprawling pine trees and crumbling boulders covered the rugged cliff tops. In the distance, twin mountains, black as the night, towered over the cliffs like silent sentinels. The peak of the eastern mountain eclipsed its western sibling by a mere boulder or two.

The island was more terrifying than Whisker had ever imagined. Even from a distance, he could hear the wind howling through the trees, roaring and racing down the cliffs to the surging sea. Closing his eyes, he imagined he was listening to a graveyard of phantoms, endlessly wailing, eternally cursed.

If the wind was the terrifying life force of the island, then the waves were its minions. They battered every rock, pounded every cliff face – savagely, relentlessly.

Whisker shivered. 'An island of destiny or an island of death?'

'Both,' Pete muttered. 'Every rat's destiny is death.'

Horace looked up from his net. 'Don't listen to him, Whisker. You can get us through. I know it!'

Whisker wished he shared Horace's confidence, but he couldn't shake his feeling of dread. He turned his back on the island and climbed the stairs to the helm.

'Any luck?' the Captain asked.

Whisker ran his tongue over his teeth, avoiding an answer. The Captain gripped harder on the wheel, unable to hide his frustration.

'Is the net ready, Horace?' he shouted.

'Nearly, Captain,' Horace replied. 'I just need to load it into a cannon.'

'I thought nets were for throwing?' the Captain snapped.

'Err, some nets are,' Horace said cautiously. 'But I'd prefer we trapped the creature *before* it got within throwing range!'

'Very well,' the Captain huffed. 'But be quick about it. The entrance to the lagoon is just ahead.'

Horace hurriedly stuffed the net into a cannon on the deck. Loose cords dangled out like the tentacles of an octopus.

Whisker watched apprehensively as the *Apple Pie* skirted around a rock and entered the Treacherous Sea. Huge cliffs rose to either side, unscaleable walls of stone, curving in an arc around the lagoon. Directly ahead, the protruding rocks were as large as ships and twice as tall. Not a blade of grass grew on their barren surfaces.

It was time for Whisker's decision: *left or right?*

He held the key in front of him and, imagining the island was the map, aligned the shaft with the centre of the mountains. Light sparkled through tiny rust holes in the surface of the key and filled the round hole at its base.

Whisker looked beyond the cliffs, beyond the rocks, beyond the lagoon to the only glimmer of beauty on the entire island: the Rock of Hope. He could just make out the shape – a white rock, bathed in sunlight and surrounded by flowing water.

He lowered the key but kept his gaze. His line of sight led directly through a narrow passage between the rocks.

'Keep Hope in your sights,' Whisker thought aloud. And then it came to him. 'Of course. The riddle is meant to be taken *literally.* There's only one way to keep Hope in our sights and that's …'

'Right or left?' the Captain bellowed. 'I need an answer.'

'Neither!' Whisker shouted. 'Sail straight ahead!'

'WHAT?' Pete cried from the deck. 'We'll be wrecked on the rocks!'

'Beaten to breadcrumbs!' Mr Tribble gasped.

'Pounded into pancakes!' Emmie squeaked.

Fred licked his lips. 'Mmm, pancakes ...'

Pete kicked Fred with his pencil. 'You're not helping! None of you are helping.' He pointed a bony finger up at Whisker. 'Give me one logical reason why we should listen to you? And it better not involve that blasted riddle. It's led to nothing but trouble!'

Whisker dropped his chin and stared at his toes.

'I don't know,' he mumbled. 'Maybe the water is too shallow for the creature ... or maybe it's too narrow between the rocks ... or maybe the wind is calmer ...'

'Three great reasons,' Horace chimed in. 'I'm convinced. Off we go then.'

Pete stamped his pencil leg in defiance. 'Call a vote, Captain.'

The Captain studied the faces of his crew and nodded. 'As you know, only full members of the crew are permitted to vote. All those in favour of sailing straight through the rocks raise your paws now.'

Horace and Fred raised their paws. Smudge stuck four arms into the air and blew off the barrel. Ruby gave Whisker one of her expressionless stares and raised her paw.

'Four votes seals it,' the Captain confirmed.

Pete snorted in disgust and clomped into the navigation room. Whisker mouthed an awkward *thanks* to Ruby, and turned to the Captain. The Captain hadn't shifted his paws from the wheel, not even to vote, and the *Apple Pie* was already heading straight into the rocks.

'You said straight,' he said in a low voice. 'I sailed straight. The vote was merely a formality.'

'Do you honestly think we can make it through?' Whisker asked.

'It's a tight squeeze,' the Captain said, 'but you were right about the wind. It's much calmer in here.'

Whisker wondered if the Captain was simply being polite. The wind swirled in mighty gusts around him, whipping up the waves and sending them crashing over the rocks. The *Apple Pie* rocked up and down in the centre of the narrow passage like a rubber duck in a bath tub.

'A little to your starboard, Captain,' Ruby called out. 'I can see the bottom and there's a rock ledge coming up.'

The Captain gave the wheel a gentle spin and the ship turned to its right.

'Pull in the sails,' he ordered. 'Too much speed and we'll collide with a rock.'

The twins tinkered with their mice knots, adjusting the sails, and the *Apple Pie* slowed its pace. Whisker held up the key. The Rock of Hope was still in view.

The crew remained alert and on edge as the *Apple Pie* manoeuvred through the rocks. Fred and Smudge stood lookout on either side of the ship, surveying the ocean; Horace waited next to the loaded cannon and Pete remained in the navigation room, doing whatever grumpy quartermasters do on such occasions.

Large rocks to the east sheltered the ship from the wind, but the swirling gusts returned with greater force as the *Apple Pie* neared the Rock of Hope.

Pete poked his head from the navigation room.

'Are we there yet?' he muttered in a less than pleasant

voice.

'Shallow water dead ahead!' Ruby cried.

Whisker looked up. The *Apple Pie* approached two final rocks. One lay to his near left, and the other further to his right.

'Turn her starboard, Captain,' he said. 'We can squeeze between the rocks and still maintain our course.'

Smudge buzzed his wings frantically and pointed to the starboard side of the ship.

'What is it?' Horace asked with wide eyes.

Ruby darted to the bulwark.

'More rocks!' she exclaimed. 'Just below the surface – everywhere. We'll run aground!'

'That can't be!' Whisker cried. 'The map says ...'

'... nothing about low tide,' Pete cut in.

Whisker looked ahead to the shore. A long strip of wet sand extended from the Rock of Hope to the sea. The tide was fully out. He felt his tail work itself into a knot.

'Rotten pies to low tide,' Horace groaned.

Pete screwed up his nose. 'Port side, Captain. Circle around the rocks. Before we bottom out.'

The Captain let out a low growl. 'Yet again, it seems we have no other choice. If we maintain a narrow berth around the rock on the left, we can hopefully centre up for the final approach.'

Whisker didn't respond. His eyes were transfixed on the rocky shape, rising like a tombstone from the crashing waves. He wasn't superstitious, but anyone could see it was a bad omen – a *very* bad omen.

'SAILS OUT!' the Captain bellowed, swinging the wheel hard left. 'And make it snappy! I want us past that rock in sixty seconds.'

The crew rushed to the sails and began to work the ropes.

'Whisker, I need you on the jib!' Ruby shouted.

Whisker leapt down the stairs and raced to the bow of the ship, still clutching the key in his paws. While Ruby and the mice adjusted the two larger sails, Whisker added some slack to the giant pair of underpants.

He edged along the bowsprit and peered down. The shallow rocks beneath the surface suddenly disappeared as the *Apple Pie* glided over the edge of a deep ravine. He looked ahead to see the Rock of Hope vanish behind the black pillar of rock. Like a solar eclipse on midsummer's day, their guiding light was gone – the Pie Rats were at the mercy of the Treacherous Sea.

'Prepare to turn,' the Captain commanded.

The crew heaved on the ropes, swivelling the sails around to capture the gusty wind. The *Apple Pie* began curving around the rock.

Seconds passed and Whisker grew anxious. He watched as the tip of the shoreline grew visible, the sand glowing yellow in the afternoon sunshine.

Almost there … Whisker thought.

The western side of the estuary came into view and then, finally, Whisker saw what he was looking for. As the *Apple Pie* straightened up, the Rock of Hope reappeared from behind the last rock of the lagoon.

Whisker sighed with relief. The eclipse was over. In moments they would be in the safety of the shallows.

THUD!

Out of nowhere, a monstrous blow echoed through the hull of the ship, toppling barrels and shattering windows. Whisker grabbed the jib line to steady himself. Behind him, Pete slipped on his pencil and tumbled onto the deck. The mice squeaked in terror.

The vibrations stopped and the crew grew silent, listening attentively to the sounds of the sea. All they heard was the deck of the *Apple Pie* creaking softly and the sails flapping quietly in the wind.

'Oh my precious paws,' Pete groaned, staggering to his feet. 'What the flaming rat's tail was that?'

Horace gripped the cannon with a terrified look on his face. 'Th-th-the creature.'

Whisker peered into the dark water at the front of the ship, hoping the hull had simply scraped a rock. Fred scanned the starboard side for clues. They saw nothing.

'Check the hull for damage ...' the Captain began. He never finished his sentence.

There was a loud *SPLASH* from the port side of the ship and an enormous head rose from the waves. Its brown-speckled skin glistened in the dying rays of the sun, its beady eyes stared down from either side of its hideous snout and its mouth curved open to reveal not one but two sets of savage jaws.

It was the most terrifying creature Whisker had ever seen. It wasn't a beast of mythology. It was real, very real and Whisker didn't need a second look to know what it was.

'GIANT MORAY EEL!' he bellowed. 'PORT SIDE!'

The eel's slender body rose higher into the air, propelled by its serpentine tail. Its dorsal fin rippled along its spine like seaweed in a tidal current. It hovered over the ship. Then it struck. Teeth bared, it ripped through the foresail.

Ruby and Mr Tribble leapt clear as the eel's body

battered the mast. The huge fork toppled backwards, tearing the jib sail from its line. Whisker was flung from the bowsprit and hurtled towards the deck.

He threw his paws forward to break his impact but the force of the landing catapulted the key from his paws. He watched in horror as it spun through the air, bounced off the bulwark, and disappeared into a shower of spray.

A moment later, the eel's enormous tail crashed onto the deck, dragging the front of the ship under the waves. Whisker struggled to stay afloat as the surge of water engulfed him. He heard the screams of the twins, desperately clutching the mainmast, and glimpsed the black figure of the Captain tumbling from the helm.

The eel's tail slid over the bulwark and the bow of the ship catapulted upwards in a wave of water. Spitting out salt water, Whisker somersaulted through the air, landed on his backside and skidded to a halt on the slippery boards.

He raised his nose and frantically scanned the deck for the key. It was nowhere in sight. Before Whisker could pick himself up, the eel had reared its vicious head out of the sea.

A loud *BOOM* echoed in Whisker's left ear and a crude net of ropes and sinkers exploded from Horace's cannon. The stray ends of long ropes snagged on broken barrels and twisted around the fallen mast. The rest of the net shot upwards, smothering the eel's head in a mass of knotted cords.

The enraged creature snapped its jaws, trying to tear through the net, but the ropes coiled around its teeth and held fast. In a fury, it lowered its head and plunged under the waves.

Barrels and boards tumbled overboard. Tangled ropes tightened. With a hard tug, the eel began dragging the *Apple Pie* away from the shore.

Whisker heard a loud cry and turned to see the Captain sliding towards a gaping hole in the bulwark, struggling to free his ankle from one of the ropes.

Panic-stricken, Whisker scrambled to his feet and threw his arms forward in a desperate attempt to grab the Captain. His paws clutched at thin air.

The rope dragged the Captain closer to the edge and, with a horrified gasp from Ruby, he vanished over the side.

There was a muffled cry and then a splash. A moment later there was a second splash as Whisker dived, headfirst, into the ocean after him.

THREE

Deep Water

The water beneath the surface was dark and turbulent. Weighed down by his sword, Whisker exhaled the air from his lungs and kicked deeper. He knew he only had seconds to find the Captain.

A black shape moved swiftly past him, covered in a tangle of criss-crossed cords. Frantically, he made a lunge for it. His paws wrapped around the smooth sides of a barrel. He dug his claws into the soft wood to stop himself slipping and held on tight. It wasn't the Captain, but it was moving in the right direction.

With the water rushing past his eyes, it was a struggle for Whisker to see anything, but he could just make out the silhouette of the *Apple Pie* above him and the shadow of a large rock to his left.

The cord jerked violently to the left and the barrel scraped the side of the rock. Whisker felt something brush past his right ear. Tightening his grip, he turned to see the limp body of the Captain drifting beside him, the rope still attached to his ankle.

Whisker seized his opportunity and grabbed the rope with one paw, looping his tail around the Captain's leg. When he was confident he was secure, he kicked off from

34

the barrel, sending it bouncing into the rock. It smashed open on impact, clouding the water in a dark liquid. Whisker lost sight of everything in the murky haze.

Frantically, he tried to draw his scissor sword, but the speed of the current worked against him. He felt for the Captain's sword. Alas, the handle was out of reach.

A burning sensation spread through his lungs and he knew he was running out of time. If the Captain was still alive, he needed to get him to the surface – fast.

The rope jolted left and Whisker was thrown against a rock. He winced in pain as a sharp piece of coral dug into his side, and he struggled not to inhale a lungful of gravy-tainted water. His head pounded, his chest burned, but he tried to stay focused.

You've survived this before, he told himself, fumbling blindly with the rope in a futile attempt to unravel twisted loops and tangled knots. It was hopeless. The knots were too tight.

Please, please, please, he begged, not giving in.

As if responding to his plea, the rope suddenly went slack and Whisker felt a surge of hope – *we're free.*

He kicked furiously with his legs and pulled himself up the side of the rock with his paw, dragging the Captain with him. The water cleared and the *Apple Pie* grew visible. Halfway to the surface the rope began to tighten.

We're still attached, he thought in panic.

In a final desperate attempt to free the Captain, Whisker looped the rope around a small outcrop of rock. Clutching the loose end in both paws, he waited in agony, his lungs ablaze.

The rope went taught, tightening the loop. The creature pulled and Whisker held on. Seconds passed. The rope refused to break. Whisker felt himself blacking out …

SNAP!

With a powerful jolt that threw Whisker backwards, the rope finally tore in two and the Captain was free. Whisker fought his way to the surface, bursting through the white crest of a wave. He gulped in the salty air, each breath more painful than the last.

Deliriously, he dragged the Captain onto a rock and reached down to check his pulse. Whisker's paw barely touched his neck when the Captain coughed up a mouthful of water and began sucking in air.

Whisker slumped down next to him, overwhelmed with relief and exhaustion. He watched helplessly as the wreck of the *Apple Pie* was dragged along the western side of the lagoon and disappeared out to sea. The Captain was alive but the Pie Rats were gone.

The black velvet hat of the Captain drifted through the waves, rising and falling like a cork in a sea of champagne. Its golden pie insignia caught the attention of the two rats on the rocks.

Whisker drew his scissor sword and plucked the soggy shape from the sea, handing it to the Captain. The Captain wedged the once-regal hat on his head, dribbling water over his face. He didn't blink. He didn't speak.

Whisker returned his sword to his belt, noticing the small map canister wedged beneath his pie-buckled belt. Its presence was a relief, but it also filled him with guilt. What good was the map without the key – the key he'd lost?

You should have been more careful, he scolded himself.

You could have put it in a pocket, or left it in the navigation room.

He sat on a rock and wallowed in guilt. The Captain hadn't spoken a word since Whisker had dragged him from the ocean, but Whisker could feel his black eye watching him closely. The key was Whisker's responsibility. This was the second time he'd lost it and there were no excuses. He had to come clean.

'I-I dropped the key in the lagoon,' he blurted out. 'I'm sorry.'

The Captain remained expressionless. 'You risked your life to save me, Whisker. I'm hardly going to give you a lecture about losing a key.'

Whisker sighed and turned back to the ocean.

'Thank you,' the Captain added. 'You didn't have to come after me. It was more than anyone could have asked. I'm supposed to be keeping *you* alive, remember?'

Whisker was unsure how to respond.

'I kind of just fell in,' he replied humbly, . 'Besides, what's an apprentice without a captain?'

'What's a captain without his crew?' the Captain said, the smile draining from his face. 'Or his ship?' He stared out at the horizon. 'You and I are two peas in a mushy pea pie, Whisker. You've lost your family and now I've lost mine.'

'B-but they'll come back for us,' Whisker stammered. 'After they escape from the eel … Ruby and Horace and the others … we'll see them again – won't we?'

The Captain put a shaky paw on Whisker's shoulder and Whisker felt a double pang of sadness in his aching chest – the Pie Rats were his family, too.

'We can only hope,' the Captain said slowly.

Whisker nodded. He was no stranger to hope. He carried it everywhere he went, in the form of a gold anchor pendant hanging around his neck. It wasn't a charm, it was a reminder.

He touched its golden surface. The faces of his parents flashed before his eyes: Faye, the green thumb, patient and kind; Robert, the circus rat, crafty and inventive. Then he saw his little sister Anna, the lover of stories, followed by the faces of the Pie Rats: Ruby, Horace, Fred, Smudge, the mice, even Pete. He couldn't give up on any of them. He *refused* to give up on any of them.

'It's getting dark,' the Captain said, breaking Whisker's thoughts. 'Do you have the energy to swim to shore?'

Whisker peered across the lagoon to the Rock of Hope, its smooth surface radiating the pink and purple hues of the twilight sky. It was a shining beacon on a rough sea. A short distance away, a barrel bobbed in the waves, and broken deck-boards and strands of rope drifted nearby.

'I can make it to the barrel,' Whisker said hoarsely. 'I think it's safer if we paddle across.'

The Captain agreed. 'Who knows what other creatures lurk beneath these waters?'

The two rats anxiously rowed their barrel-boat across the choppy surface of the lagoon. Fortunately, there were no signs of giant eels, stinging bluebottles or hungry fish.

They reached the sandy shallows, slid from the barrel and dragged themselves onto the shore. It wasn't the triumphant landing Whisker had hoped for, but he had finally reached the Island of Destiny.

Grateful to be alive, he squeezed the water from his clothes and staggered up the sand. The Captain limped beside him, wincing with every step. From the safety of their spiral shells, hermit crabs watched the waterlogged rats approach the Rock of Hope.

Whisker knelt down in the centre of the estuary and drank from the cool water flowing around the rock. It was pure and thirst-quenching and tasted refreshingly sweet after the salty water of the ocean.

With renewed strength, he stood up and stared at the giant rock in the centre of the river. In the fading light, it appeared as a ball of pale blue, framed by the black silhouettes of the twin mountains. Whisker could hear the wind howling through the foothills and the waves crashing against the cliffs. The Rock of Hope was like the calm eye of a cyclone – a place of peace in the midst of its turbulent surroundings.

He saw a flicker of movement from the upper edge of the rock. When he looked again, it was gone. He scanned the estuary, puzzled.

'Is something wrong?' the Captain asked with a furrowed brow.

'No,' Whisker said. 'I thought I saw … oh, never mind.'

The Captain glanced warily at the rock. 'I suggest we head into the foothills and find shelter for the night. The further we are from the lagoon, the safer I'll feel.'

The two rats followed the beach past the Rock of Hope and ascended a grass-covered dune to the east. The wind raced over the crest, spraying grains of sand into their eyes. Whisker raised his arm to protect his face and squeezed his eyes until they were almost shut.

Blindly, they pressed on.

The dune dropped down into a sandy valley and then rose to meet a line of sprawling pine trees. Whisker scrambled up the bank, his toes sinking into the sand. The

Captain trudged warily beside him, his eye darting from the trees to the dunes.

They'd almost reached the crooked trunk of a huge pine tree, when the Captain threw out his arm and stopped Whisker in his tracks.

'Stay perfectly still,' he hissed.

Whisker froze.

'What is it?' he whispered.

The Captain sniffed the air and moved his paw to the handle of his sword.

'Something's following us,' he said in a low voice. 'Don't turn around – not until I give the signal, understand?'

'Y-yes, Captain,' Whisker trembled.

Cautiously, the rats entered the pine forest, their eyes adjusting to the gloom. The wind whistled above them, and dry needles crackled under their feet. Their pursuer was silent.

As they moved further into the forest, the dense canopy of branches and pine needles blocked the faint light of evening stars. Whisker caught a strong scent of onion in the air and stopped. The Captain pulled him behind a tree and drew his sword.

'It's here,' he whispered, 'whatever it is …'

'What do we do?' Whisker asked, hoping the creature was nothing more than a large onion rolling along in the wind.

The Captain felt the rough, flaking bark of the tree.

'We either fight the beast or climb and hope our pursuer has vertigo,' he said. 'What's it to be?'

Whisker drew his sword. Although he was still a novice at sword fighting, he'd already faced Sabre, the dreaded captain of the Cat Fish, and survived. Cowering in a tree

40

didn't seem like a Pie Rat thing to do.

There was a soft *crunch* from the opposite side of the tree. The Captain pointed at Whisker and gestured to his left, his fingers twitching on the handle of his scissor sword.

Whisker nodded.

The Captain raised three fingers and then lowered them, silently counting, *three … two … one … NOW!*

The rats attacked. Swords raised, they leapt from either side of the tree to face their enemy. The forest floor was deserted, but the onion smell lingered. Back to back, Whisker and the Captain scanned their surrounds for any sign of life.

'It must be close,' the Captain whispered. 'Watch your feet for hidden burrows …'

Suddenly there was a loud cackling sound from the branches above him and Whisker jumped in fright.

'Noisy sailors choose to *fight,*' laughed a thin, raspy voice. 'Hermit chooses to *climb*. Sailors never catch Hermit in a tree. Hermit knows forest like eel knows lagoon.'

Trembling, Whisker peered up, unable to see anything through the mass of needles and pine cones overhead. The Captain slashed at low branches in frustration.

'Reveal yourself, you devilish fiend!' he shouted. 'If that vile sea creature is a pet of yours, you'll pay dearly, do you hear?'

'No! No!' the voice cried. 'Nasty eel is not Hermit's pet. Eel is no one's pet!'

'So why were you following us?' the Captain roared.

'Hermit was curious,' the voice croaked. 'Hermit not seen pesky visitors on island for many y –' he stopped himself and laughed. 'Hermit not seen visitors on island

– ever!'

The Captain was far from amused.

'We're not visitors to be trifled with,' he hissed. 'Our scissor swords are sharp and ...'

'Scissor swords?' the voice broke in. 'Noisy sailors carry scissor swords: sparkling, shiny scissor swords? Sailors let harmless old Hermit hold one, yes, yes? Just for a moment?'

'Not on your life!' the Captain bellowed. 'The closest you'll come to a scissor sword is when my blade is pointed at your conniving throat!'

The voice in the tree didn't respond. Whisker felt an icy gust of wind blow through the forest.

'Stay alert,' the Captain whispered.

Awaiting an attack, Whisker raised his sword above his head and scanned the darkness for the mysterious pursuer.

There was a dull thud to his right. The Captain leapt in the direction of the sound but Whisker stayed rooted to the spot, his tail squirming in the pine needles at his feet.

The onion smell drifted into his nostrils.

'He's not there,' the Captain hissed over his shoulder.

'I know,' Whisker said in a petrified voice. 'He's standing right behind me.'

The Captain spun around – and abruptly halted. An expression of pure bewilderment ran across his face.

'You!' he gasped.

Whisker slowly turned. A scrawny rat stood in the shadows of the trees, his sinewy body draped in a course, fibrous cloak. He was a rat of many years, lean and ragged, but a match for any rat – scissor sword or not. His black eyes sparkled with a familiar intensity, though Whisker

42

was certain he'd never seen him before.

Defensively, Whisker tightened the grip on his weapon and maintained his stance. The rat stared past Whisker to the Captain, a look of recognition filling his eyes. A broad smile grew across his face.

'Many moons have passed,' he sighed. 'Yes, yes. Time has been long.'

'Not long enough,' the Captain said through gritted teeth.

The Hermit's smile quickly vanished. He looked at Whisker with desperate eyes. Whisker took a step backwards, aware this was no ordinary reunion.

The Captain extended his sword and scowled. 'Ran out of gold, did you, *Hermit*? Decided to return to the island to finish your failed quest?'

The Hermit's jaw dropped. His lip trembled.

Whisker turned from the Hermit to the Captain and suddenly it clicked.

'Return?' the Hermit gasped. 'No, no. Hermit could never return. Hermit never left!'

FOUR

The Hermit

Captain Black Rat had a temper but he wasn't a fool. The fire died in his eye as quickly as it had sparked.

He lowered his sword and stared, transfixed, at the strange figure in front of him. The Hermit stared back, motionless. Both rats shared the same expression – disbelief.

'But Rat Bait said …' the Captain choked.

'Rat Bait said many things,' the Hermit murmured. 'Many stories, many tales, yes, yes. But truth? Hmm …' He took a deep breath. 'Hermit remembers stormy afternoon, wild, wild sea. Eel attacked *Princess Pie*. Hermit tumbled overboard. *Princess Pie* vanished into storm. Hermit waited months – Hermit waited years. Crew of *Princess Pie* never returned …'

He pointed to the map canister in Whisker's belt. 'Hermit left Forgotten Map for his son.' He turned back to the Captain. 'Finally you have come.'

The Captain looked from the Hermit to Whisker, his face a sea of emotions.

'The map was meant for *me*?' he gasped in confusion. 'My father was here all along … But-but that means everything Rat Bait told us was a lie.'

Whisker searched his mind for clarity, trying to separate *truth* from *treachery*. He remembered the night he'd met Rat Bait, the former first mate of the *Princess Pie*, and recalled the words the old rogue had spoken. One line of Rat Bait's story suddenly took on a whole new meaning: *We lost the c – we lost the cargo and supplies over the side.*

At the time, Whisker was fixated on the treasure and thought nothing of Rat Bait's awkward pause. But now it was obvious. Rat Bait had almost given himself away. The *Princess Pie* hadn't lost her *cargo*, she had lost her *captain*.

'We know Rat Bait lied about the key,' Whisker said quietly. 'There's nothing to stop him lying about your father, too.'

The Hermit gave the Captain a pleading stare. The Captain stared back, speechless. His tongue moved, but he didn't utter a sound.

Whisker could only imagine what was going through his mind. The very rat the Captain had trained himself to hate was standing right in front of him, no longer a monster but an innocent victim of a terrible lie.

After an agonising silence, the Captain slowly extended the handle of his scissor sword to the Hermit, struggling to hold back the tears.

'A noble captain deserves a sword,' he quavered, 'and the loyalty of his family.'

The Hermit took one look at the sword and threw his arms around the Captain.

'Hermit needs his *son*,' he sobbed.

For a moment, the Captain stood rigid, then, with a gush of tears, he dropped his sword and hugged the Hermit tightly. The Hermit pounded the Captain on the back like a giddy school boy celebrating a winning goal. The sobbing soon turned to laughter.

Whisker watched the joyous reunion, unable to look away. Part of him felt like an outsider, but the rest of him longed to know what it felt like to finally have his family back. He'd come to the island with high hopes. The Island of Destiny had already rewritten one future.

The Captain finally broke from the Hermit's embrace and regained his composure.

'Whisker,' he said in a formal voice, 'may I present to you my father, Ratsputin, noble captain of the *Princess Pie* and Pie Rat extraordinaire!'

The Hermit

The Hermit extended his paw to Whisker and spoke with oniony breath. 'Hermit pleased to meet you, master Whisker.'

Whisker shook his rough paw. 'The pleasure is mine, Captain Ratsputin, sir.'

The Hermit twitched his ears. 'Captain Ratsputin, no, no. *Hermit* it is. No captain here, only Hermit, scorpions and owls.' He waved his arms theatrically above his head. 'Hermit welcomes you to windy, windy island where wind is always windy!'

'Nice to, err … be here,' Whisker replied, wondering if the Hermit had spent a little too long in the sun – or the wind.

The Hermit gave him a long stare and waved his finger in a circle around his ear.

'Hermit not cuckoo,' he laughed. 'Hermit just muddles words. Hermit not used to visitors. Owls and scorpions not friendly neighbours, no, no!' He lowered his voice and looked around suspiciously. 'Owls hunt at night. Must hurry. Hermit's lair this way.'

He took a step into the undergrowth and beckoned for them to follow. The Captain picked up his sword and gave Whisker a reassuring nod. Together, the two Pie Rats followed the Hermit into the darkness of the forest.

The ground rose steadily upwards as the Hermit marched on, leading the rats further from the lagoon. The sandy dirt of the forest floor became rockier and the pine trees turned to mountain shrubs. Moss-covered boulders dotted the dark landscape, heralding the foothills of the mighty twin mountains. The sound of running water echoed in the distance.

The Hermit stopped next to a small plant, bent down

and wrapped his fingers around its thin, green stem. Giving it a sharp tug, a brown onion bulb popped up from the dry earth. He brushed the soil from the onion and continued up the slope, quietly whistling to himself.

The sound of water grew louder and a gurgling brook came into view, meandering past rocks and bushes. Starlight sparkled across its rippling surface. Whisker stopped, hypnotised by its gentle rhythm.

'River flows from mountain spring,' the Hermit whispered, moving steadily away from the river. Hermit's lair on eastern mountain, Mt Moochup. Keep moving. No time to waste!'

Whisker pulled his eyes from the enchanting stream and trailed after him. Soon they were in the open, scrambling up egg-shaped boulders and creeping through crevices on the lower slopes of the mountain. The wind tore through their clothes. Whisker pushed his body close to the rocks, hoping the next icy gust wouldn't carry him away.

He looked to the air for any sign of owls. The rocky peaks of the mountains spiralled upwards towards the starry heavens and a dark ring of cliffs surrounded the lagoon far below.

The Hermit vanished into a crevice and Whisker and the Captain shuffled after him, entering the onion-scented interior of a small cave.

With a *TAP* of two stones, a spark flashed in the darkness. Several taps later and the Hermit had managed to start a small fire in the centre of the cave. He threw a bundle of dried grass and sticks onto the fire and chuckled, 'Owls don't see smoke on windy nights, no, no! Hermit has *roast* onions on windy nights, yes, yes.'

He proceeded to gather an armful of small onions from a pile in the corner and handed several to Whisker and the Captain.

'Onions and pine nuts – island delicacies!' he said, taking a seat next to the fire. 'Roast pine nuts for dessert.'

The Hermit peeled an onion and wedged it on the end of a stick. The others watched as he began turning it over the flames.

Whisker generally disliked brown onions. His mother once told him they were packed with essential vitamins, but that hardly compensated for their terrible aftertaste. On this occasion, however, hunger and good manners ensured he gave at least one a try. He figured it would be impolite to ask for dessert before he'd touched his main course.

Hesitantly, he selected the smallest onion from the pile and tore off its outer layers. Following the Hermit's lead, he skewered the onion on a stick and thrust it into the fire.

The smell of roast onions was surprisingly appetising. Whisker ate three well-cooked onions and several pawfuls of roasted pine nuts before his hunger was satisfied. He leant back against a rock and hoped it was only *raw* onions that gave the Hermit his terrible breath. A loud oniony burp that popped out of his own mouth quickly convinced him otherwise.

'It's a good thing Ruby's not here,' he muttered quietly to himself. 'But then again ...'

The Hermit's ears twitched.

'Who's Ruby?' he asked inquisitively.

'Ruby is our boatswain,' the Captain said. 'She's also my dear niece and your granddaughter.'

'Hermit has a granddaughter?' the Hermit exclaimed.

The Captain nodded. 'She's a fine girl, our Ruby. Isn't she, Whisker?'

Whisker felt his cheeks flushing.

'Y-yes,' he stammered.

'Ruby lost her mother, your daughter, in the plague, along with the rest of her family,' the Captain explained to the Hermit. 'Ruby's been in my crew ever since she was old enough to swing a sword.'

The Hermit's face darkened. 'Little Lilith is gone?'

'Yes, I'm sorry,' the Captain said. 'Many things have changed over the years.'

'Hermit's wife?' the Hermit asked.

The Captain grinned. 'Granny Rat is as angry as ever and very much alive. She'll be furious to see you, that's for sure. But I've no doubt she'll welcome you back with open arms.' His face grew stern. 'Granny never trusted Rat Bait and often questioned his story. Heaven help the lying scoundrel if she ever tracks him down – if *I* ever track him down.'

'Hermit is afraid we'll never see any of them again,' the Hermit said gravely. 'Ships never return to windy, windy island. Hermit and rats stranded forever.'

Whisker's tail coiled itself around an onion. The Captain gave the Hermit a defiant look, as if accepting a challenge.

'You don't know the crew of the *Apple Pie*,' he murmured. 'They're loyal to the end. If they're alive, they'll return. I know it.'

'Hermit hopes so,' the Hermit sighed. 'Hermit once believed *Princess Pie* would return. Every day he watched. Every day the same: empty horizon.'

'Except today,' the Captain said.

''Cept today,' the Hermit repeated. 'Today more rats

marooned ...'

The Captain didn't respond. The Hermit sighed and threw another branch on the fire, its withered leaves bursting into flames. Whisker looked from the Hermit to the Captain, sensing it was going to be a stalemate.

'So what can *we* do?' he asked in a small voice. 'Surely we can build a raft to get off the island?'

The Hermit brushed the ash off his paws. 'Hermit built raft, yes, yes. Many years ago. Mighty raft it was – wrecked on Cyclone Sea. Hermit swam back to island.'

'What about the treasure?' Whisker asked hopefully. 'We know it has great power.'

The Hermit shook his head.

'Treasure still a mystery,' he replied sadly. 'Hermit searched for many years on western mountain. Hermit found no clue of secret location.'

Whisker glanced guiltily at the Captain and then turned back to the Hermit.

'The King's Key revealed where the treasure was hidden,' he explained, 'but I'm afraid it's lying at bottom of the Treacherous Sea.'

The Hermit's eyes lit up. 'Whisker remembers location of treasure?'

'Yes,' Whisker replied. 'The lower slopes of Mt Mobziw. But a location's not much good without the key. I'm sure we'll need it to open a door or ...'

'Whisker shows Hermit the map!' the Hermit cut in. 'Hermit shows Whisker something – useful.'

'Oh-ok,' Whisker said, intrigued.

He reached across for the map canister, drying near the fire and carefully removed its delicate contents. The Hermit shuffled to the back of the cave and pulled out a brown drawstring bag from a crack in the wall. He brought the bag closer to the fire.

'Hermit's treasures,' he said, reaching his paw inside.

He pulled out an ancient compass, a few scraps of faded paper and a rusty metal key. Like a mother handling a new born baby, he gently placed them on a rock.

Whisker cautiously picked up the key and examined it closely. It had three teeth and an oval shaped handle. Its rough, iron surface lacked any painted detail, but its outline was unmistakable. With growing excitement, he placed it over the hole in the map. It was an exact fit.

'Well I'll be ...' he marvelled.

'So you had a key after all, you crafty sea dog!' the Captain chuckled.

The Hermit winked. 'Hermit made key from outline on map many years ago. Hermit no fool, no, no! Hermit just bad at solving riddles to locate real key.'

The Captain laughed. 'That's why it pays to have a bright young apprentice in your crew!' He slapped Whisker on the back. 'This one's quite the problem solver when he's not wrestling chameleons or infuriating giant spider crabs.'

The Hermit grinned at Whisker. 'Many problems for apprentice to solve on windy, windy island, yes, yes. Hermit takes rats to Mt Mobziw – first light. Now rats sleep.'

Almost on cue, Whisker let out a deep yawn. His mind was still racing, but his body longed for rest. It had been a big day – most days were big days with the Pie Rats. Whisker had lost count of how many days he had nearly died, had nearly been eaten or had nearly died while nearly being eaten. Reassuring himself he was at least safe for the night, he curled up next to the fire and, with one last oniony burp, fell fast asleep.

FIVE

X Marks the Spot

awn was just as windy as the night before. Whisker awoke to the sound of the wind whistling through the narrow entrance to the cave. Through the thin wisps of smoke circling around the smouldering fire, he saw the Hermit shuffling along the wall, munching on a raw onion like it was a juicy apple.

Whisker sat up and wiped the sleep from his eyes. His troubled dreams had been filled with scenes of sinking ships and drowning rats, but the nightmares faded from his mind when he saw the first rays of the rising sun.

Today we search for the treasure, he told himself. *Today I find my answer.*

He scoffed down a rushed breakfast of cold nuts, politely refusing the raw onion on offer, and set off with the others towards Mt Mobziw. The Hermit had a spring in his step. The Captain had a spring and a slight hobble. Whisker scurried.

They traversed the rough ground, heading west. The land dropped away to the south, exposing the rocky faces of huge boulders. The Rock of Hope, clearly visible on the sandy lip of the lagoon, glowed a rich gold in the morning sun.

Whisker searched the sea for ships. Crashing waves and jagged rocks filled his vision. He could see the Hermit up ahead, staring at the same distant scene, and wondered how many days the marooned rat had spent watching and waiting for a ship to sail into view.

Thousands, he guessed. *Are we destined to wait for thousands more?*

The rats continued marching until they were directly above a stream of water gushing from a hole in the mountainside. The water splashed over the rocks to form a shallow river, twisting its way down the slope towards the ocean.

'Mountain spring,' the Hermit whispered. 'Centre of windy, windy island. River runs south to white rock.' He pointed ahead. 'Mt Mobziw west, Mt Moochup east. Scorpions north, yes, yes! Rats hurry past.'

They continued at a faster pace, Whisker keeping a watchful eye to the north. Scorpions, together with giant spider crabs, were at the top of his list of *creepy critters to avoid at all costs*.

Whisker was by nature a climber. The Hermit, it seemed, was a rock-hopper. He leapt between boulders like they were nothing more than cobblestones on a flat road, perfectly timing his jumps over crevices and small ravines so his pace never altered. He moved so swiftly and silently along the rocks that Whisker and the Captain almost lost sight of him.

After hours of frantic scrambling, the rats began moving higher up the side of the mountain. The terrain transformed from smooth-topped boulders to crumbling black rocks and loose soil. The occasional wind-ravaged pine tree punctuated the bleak landscape.

The Hermit stopped and waited for the others to catch up.

'Owl territory,' he said in a matter-of-fact voice. 'Whisker checks map, yes, yes?'

Whisker added *owls* to his mental list and slid the map from the canister. He held it steady in the wind as the Hermit took the rusty key from his bag.

The Captain used his fingernail to scratch a small X on the lower tooth, replicating the treasure symbol from the original King's Key. The Hermit's eyes grew wide with delight as the Captain moved the key into position over the map.

'According to these coordinates,' the Captain explained, 'the treasure should be located halfway along the mountain, just above the line of boulders.' He glanced around at the mountainside. 'We must be close.'

The Hermit twitched his ears. 'Not here, no, no. Further west. Hermit knows the way.'

He grabbed the key from the Captain's paw and excitedly raced off up the mountain. Whisker and the Captain were left staring after him.

'He hasn't changed a bit,' the Captain chuckled to Whisker. 'Not even the island has slowed him down. He's the same fearless and energetic rat I remember when I was a boy – a little rash and impulsive, mind you, but that comes with the territory.'

Whisker could see the sheer joy on the Captain's face as he revisited his childhood memories – memories he'd suppressed for many years. It seemed a wall of hatred had finally been dissolved.

The Hermit glanced over his shoulder and hooted down to them like an owl. 'Hurry, hurry. Slow rats are owl's breakfast. Lazy rats are scorpion's tea!'

Whisker stashed the map in his belt and jogged after the Hermit with the Captain laughing by his side.

'Remind you of anyone?' the Captain asked playfully.

'I can think of one fearless, energetic and impulsive rat,' Whisker replied. 'Though *she* comes with a temper!'

'An unfortunate family trait,' the Captain sighed. 'You can thank Granny Rat for that. She's got more angst than Ruby, yours truly and a giant moray eel put together!' He stroked his chin thoughtfully. 'On saying that, Granny does make a terrific mashed potato pie when she's in a rage. It's to die for!'

'Potato pie!' the Hermit moaned from up ahead. 'What Hermit would give for mashed potato pie!'

Reaching the supposed treasure site, Whisker half expected to find a giant X painted on the side of the mountain. It turned out there was no X, no hidden door and nothing whatsoever to indicate they were remotely close to the treasure.

The Hermit was convinced their location matched the bearing on the map, but after many hours of scraping through dirt and tapping on rocks, he too began to have his doubts.

'We're missing something,' Whisker remarked for the seventeenth time that afternoon.

'Clearly,' the Captain said in frustration.

The Hermit put down his sharpened stick and clambered out of the hole he'd been digging. He wandered over to where the map lay spread on the ground, its edges weighed down by four small stones.

Staring at the map for some time, he read the last two lines of the riddle aloud.

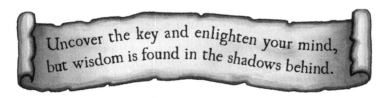

Uncover the key and enlighten your mind,
but wisdom is found in the shadows behind.

Expectantly, the Hermit looked across at Whisker for an interpretation.

Whisker brushed the wind-swept fur out of his eyes and searched his memory.

'We already know what the last line means,' he said. 'It led us to the missing key. Well, one of them, anyway.'

The Hermit looked confused.

Whisker tried to explain. 'We found two keys in the jungle citadel. The first key, the false key, was made of gold and symbolised wealth. The second key, the King's Key, was cast from brass and represented *wisdom*. We *uncovered* the King's Key while we were searching *in the shadows behind* the citadel. It was hanging around the neck of an overly annoyed three-horned chameleon ...'

'No, no!' the Hermit said in alarm.

'We made it out alive,' the Captain reassured him. 'But it was an *explosive* experience to say the least – our master gunner, Horace, blew up half the cliff top trying to escape!'

The Hermit nodded in amusement and Whisker looked back at the riddle, pondering.

'We never did work out what *enlighten your mind* meant ...' His voice drifted off and there was a long pause.

'Perhaps we need the King's Key after all,' the Captain said, with a tinge of regret. 'I dare say there's a detail on its painted surface we somehow overlooked.'

Whisker knew the Captain wasn't laying blame, but it didn't stop a feeling of guilt overwhelming him. He thought it best he kept his mouth shut and wandered off to find another hole to dig.

He'd only scooped out a few pawfuls of dirt when he heard the Hermit approaching.

'Hermit wonders *where* key was lost in lagoon?' the Hermit asked eagerly.

Whisker had no desire to relive the experience, but

decided an honest reply would be the quickest way to end the discussion once and for all.

'I lost the key to the north-west of the last rock,' he admitted. 'It happened when the eel dragged our bow under the water. I should have been more careful, I know.'

The Hermit patted Whisker on the shoulder and gave him a reassuring smile.

'Giant eel no friendly goldfish!' he laughed. 'Not to worry. Lagoon has rocky bottom. Key waits for rats. Rats dive for key, yes, yes?'

'Err, sure,' Whisker said, not wanting to dampen the Hermit's enthusiasm. 'But what about the eel?'

'Eel not coming back, no, no,' the Hermit chuckled. 'Pie Rats took care of eel!'

Whisker was somewhat reassured by the Hermit's response, but his tail still shivered at the thought of swimming across the lagoon. Experience had taught him that even the vilest of creatures could have a mate – or a family.

The Hermit continued excitedly, 'Hermit has small rowboat, yes, yes. Driftwood hull. Seaweed camouflage. Not ocean-ready like raft but sturdy enough for lagoon. Hermit takes rats to beach.'

'Tomorrow, perhaps,' the Captain said, joining the conversation. 'It seems we've been on this mountain longer than any of us have realised.'

Whisker looked west to where the sun hung low in the sky. Clouds gathered overhead, swirling in the gusty winds.

The Hermit took one look at the brewing storm and nodded in agreement. 'Key fishing tomorrow. Boiled onions tonight!'

Treasureless, the three rats packed up their belongings and hurriedly set off towards the Hermit's lair.

SIX

Constellations

Whisker made a concerted effort to look out for wild fruits and berry bushes on his trek down the mountainside. The unpleasant aftertaste of onions still lingered from the night before and boiled *anything* was hardly a meal to look forward to.

Before long, the thick clouds had blanketed the entire sky and darkness crept in. Whisker reached a large boulder near the mountain spring and spotted a scraggly bush growing from a crevice. In the fading light, he could just see what looked like clumps of red berries dangling from its branches.

'This looks promising,' he muttered to himself.

He skipped over to investigate. The dark, spiky-tipped leaves were an instant giveaway. It was a holly bush. His heart sank in disappointment. He didn't need to be the son of a fruit and vegetable seller to know that a bellyful of holly berries would give him much more than just bad breath.

Discouraged, he stepped away from the bush and turned to go; suddenly realising he was all alone. He looked ahead but saw no one. Beginning to panic, he looked right, glanced left and peered up and down the mountain – still no one.

With a mixture of fear and annoyance, he wondered how long he'd been walking on his own, distracted by his hungry thoughts.

He shouted the names of the Hermit and the Captain, but the roar of the wind and the gushing of the stream drowned his voice. Above him, the sky looked ominous, the dark clouds a clear warning that rain could fall at any moment. Whisker had no choice but to sprint blindly along the boulders, hoping he was headed in the right direction.

Without the sun or the stars to guide him, he was forced to rely on familiar landmarks to get his bearings. It didn't help that all the boulders looked identically *unfamiliar* to him.

After running aimlessly for what seemed like hours, Whisker accepted the fact he was hopelessly lost. He sniffed the air, hoping to catch a whiff of the Hermit's onion odour, but the wind carried nothing but the salty scent of the sea.

'If only I had the Hermit's compass,' he mumbled.

There was a faint tapping sound from behind a rock. Whisker spun around, half expecting to see the Hermit sneaking up on him. What he saw was far less comforting.

The shiny black shape of a scorpion crept from the shadows. Its long, segmented tail curved high above its body, ready to strike. Its two claws stretched forward, pincers open. Eight red-tinged legs moved stealthily over the ground. Its beady eyes showed no sign of expression as it moved into striking range.

Whisker had no doubts about its intentions. It had

come to fight, not to offer directions. Realising this wasn't a moment for heroics, he turned on his heel and ran.

The scuttling of legs echoed around him. Out of the corner of his eye he glimpsed two scorpions advancing on his left. Two more appeared to his right. In front of him, flanked by two boulders, were a dozen waiting scorpions. Whisker's escape route was blocked.

Common sense told him to stop and assess his options, but fear kept his legs moving. He drew his scissor sword and tried to recall the defensive guards Ruby had taught him.

Roof Guard, he told himself, raising his sword above his head.

The first attack came from his left. With a downwards thrust of its tail, a scorpion stabbed at Whisker's chest. Whisker swung his sword through the air in a powerful arc. His blade collided with the thick exoskeleton of the scorpion, battering the sting away.

He recovered from the impact just in time to see a second sting flashing towards him. He jerked his sword upwards and in the same motion threw his body forward. His sword deflected the blow and his body rolled clear under the scorpion's tail.

The scorpion swivelled itself around and made a lunge for Whisker with its claw. Whisker grabbed the scorpion's nearest leg and pulled himself to his feet as the claw snapped shut. With a violent tug on his shorts, Whisker knew the scorpion had him.

He tried to wrench himself free. The leg of his canvas shorts tore away and he broke from the pincer's grip. Three stumbling steps later and he was up and racing again.

Whisker had the advantage of speed. But speed wasn't

much good if he was paralysed by a sting. One wrong step and it would all be over.

He drew closer to the barricade of scorpions. Two large scorpions scuttled out to intercept him. Whisker hacked at the first scorpion's legs before it had time to strike. Its legs bent beneath it and its abdomen collapsed onto the ground.

The next scorpion was ready and raised its tail in anticipation. Whisker sidestepped to the right as its sting rocketed down.

It thrust again, but this time, Whisker swung his blade through the air in a wide arc, hoping to make contact. His sword missed its mark and his body continued to spin. He felt the scorpion's tail brush past his arm, narrowly missing him with its poisonous barb.

Whisker let the movement take over. He spun a complete three hundred and sixty degrees and slashed at the tail with his next pass. This time his sword made contact and with a sharp *CRACK* he severed the poisonous tip off the sting.

The scorpion flicked its tail in fury and beat the ground wildly with its claws. Whisker darted past the enraged creature while he still had the chance.

He could hear the swarm of scorpions advancing behind him and saw the barricade only metres away. More scorpions had gathered to block the narrow space. Whisker knew that even if he reached them, he could never fight his way through.

Run or fight? he asked himself.

Before Whisker could decide which way he was going to perish, he remembered the advice of his great-grandfather, Anso – advice that had saved him more than once before:

Always look for the third option.

Whisker scanned his surroundings and, with a rush of adrenalin, seized his escape plan. It lay directly in front of him, as clear as a boulder on a mountainside.

He whipped his tail over his shoulder and wrapped it around the handle of his sword, freeing up both paws. Arching his sword over his head like the sting of a scorpion, he charged at the outermost guard. He knew he only had one shot to get it right. Imagining he was an acrobatic possum from the circus, he prepared his routine.

It's all in the timing, he told himself.

The scorpion raised its tail and Whisker increased his speed. He was three steps from the scorpion when he altered his pace, taking several short hops instead of his running strides.

Misjudging Whisker's timing, the scorpion struck too soon. It thrust its tail downwards, crashing its sting into the ground.

Whisker took his final step and leapt onto the arch of the scorpion's bent tail. The scorpion flicked its tail upwards, catapulting him into the air.

Whisker soared over the barricade of scorpions with a double somersault and landed on a rocky ledge, halfway up the side of a rough boulder. Before the scorpions realised where he had gone, Whisker had scrambled to the top of the boulder and was racing along its upper edge.

He reached the next boulder, stuck his sword in his belt and continued climbing upwards. The army of scorpions scuttled after him, but the furious snaps of their claws only spurred him on. With a newfound strength, he leapt over narrow ravines and sprinted up slopes with a pace that would rival even the Hermit.

The sounds of his pursuers grew fainter and fainter as he continued, but Whisker didn't stop moving until he was high up the mountainside and all he could hear was the roar of the wind.

As the first fat raindrops exploded around him, Whisker found shelter in a rocky crevice, covering himself with leaves and sticks to conceal his location. Thunder rumbled overhead and the heavens opened, sending an icy cocktail of rain and hail pelting down.

Whisker shuffled to the very back of the crevice to the only dry spot he could find. He tried to remain alert but his eyelids were heavy with exhaustion. The low rumble of thunder and the steady trickle of water running over the rocks finally lulled him to sleep.

It was still dark when Whisker awoke. Cautiously, he brushed the damp foliage from his body and crawled out from his hiding place. Outside, the sky was clear and dotted with stars.

He scanned the dark landscape. Pine trees, loose rocks and small boulders surrounded him. The rain had washed away any lingering scents from the previous day, but the small muddy holes in the earth told him he had found his way back to the treasure site.

He studied the constellations in the sky to get his bearings. Locating a small cross of stars above him, he moved his finger through the axis of the cross to an imaginary point in the sky.

'South,' he muttered to himself.

He swivelled his body to the west and saw the unmistakable shape of a saucepan. The *saucepan* was his favourite group of stars. No matter how lost or alone he felt, it reminded him that there was at least one family sharing dinner together, somewhere in the world. He knew the stars belonged to a constellation called Orion, but Whisker preferred the saucepan title.

'A saucepan of boiled onions,' he mused. 'That's one dinner I'm happy to have missed.'

He turned his head and looked east. The twisting constellation of Scorpio stood out against the blackness.

'Scorpions,' he shivered. 'Something else to avoid.'

He set off east in the direction of his least favourite constellation. He knew if he continued on the highest path between the two mountains, he could reach Mt Moochup and bypass the scorpions. In the light of day he could then wind his way south towards the Hermit's lair.

He was still staring up at the heavens when the stars overhead suddenly darkened. An instant later they twinkled back to life.

Whisker stopped and scanned the air. The stars to the north disappeared and then reappeared as if something had passed in front of them.

Clouds don't move that quickly, he thought. *Even on windy, windy islands. Something else is up there ...*

Whisker realised the danger too late. With a sudden rush of air, powerful talons griped his shoulders and his legs were lifted off the ground. He squeaked in alarm, but the talons only gripped him tighter. There was nothing he could do. An owl had him.

SEVEN

A Nest of Fools

Whisker watched the constellations swirl around him like a kaleidoscope of diamonds. The owl flapped its wings and soared higher.

Whisker shut his eyes tight and tried to relax his wildly twitching tail. It wasn't the height that terrified him; it was the thought of being dropped from such a height. He'd been in the air many times before, with flying foxes from the circus. But flying foxes ate fruit, not rodents.

The owl seemed determined not to release its prey, nor to squeeze Whisker to death and, after a turbulent flight, Whisker felt the woven twigs of a nest beneath his feet.

The talons released their grip and Whisker slumped onto his back. He cautiously opened one eye and looked up. The sides of a large nest rose around him. Three owls perched on its uppermost edge.

In the darkness, Whisker could just make out subtle bands of white, grey and brown feathers covering their bodies. Short tufts protruded from the owl's heads like ears. Their huge yellow eyes stared inquisitively down at him.

Whisker opened his second eye.

The owls blinked.

68

Startled by the sudden movement, Whisker lunged for his sword but the owl in the middle shot out a powerful claw and pinned his arm to the nest.

'Not a wise moooove,' hooted the owl to Whisker's right. He was the biggest of the three owls and puffed up his feathers to look even larger as he spoke.

'Of course it's not a wise moooove,' shrilled the owl on the left. 'He's a pesky rat! Whooooever heard of a rat dooooing anything wise?'

Whisker felt mildly insulted by the owl's remark, but decided it wasn't the time to start an argument about the underrated intelligence of the rat race.

The owl in the middle kept Whisker pinned down, staring hungrily at his captive.

'Can we eat him yet, mother?' he asked excitedly. 'I'm so hungry. I haven't eaten anything but bugs and slugs for weeks.'

Whisker gulped.

'Ask your father, Hoooouston!' the mother owl squawked. 'He's responsible for breakfasts. I have more than enough on my plate providing yoooou with lunches, dinners and crunchy snail snacks!'

The pupils of the biggest owl grew wide as he studied Whisker in the gloom.

'He's a bit scrawny for a proper meal, son,' he considered. 'How would yooooou feel if we ripped out his gizzards and mashed them intoooo entrée sized rat-balls?'

'I'd feel absolutely terrible!' Whisker blurted out.

'Whoooo asked yoooou?' the mother owl hooted.

'N-n-no one,' Whisker stammered. 'B-b-but I'd hate for you to make a big mistake, being so wise and all.'

'Eating breakfast is never a mistake,' Houston said pompously. 'Breakfast is the most important meal of the day. Everyone knows that.'

Whisker had no comeback. He simply stared up at the owls as a horrible realisation sank in: they were actually going to eat him and there was nothing he could do about it. He couldn't fight his way out and he couldn't argue for his release – not with three know-it-all owls hovering over him.

His eyes shifted from the owls to the saucepan constellation above their heads. Suddenly the thought of boiled onions didn't seem so bad.

Onions sure beat rat-balls, he thought, his mind drifting

off. He wondered what his parents and sister would be eating for breakfast, wherever they were. *Coconuts from a deserted island, perhaps?*

His thoughts turned to the Pie Rats, swirling in circles on their leaky boat. *Maybe they've risen for an early breakfast?* He pictured Ruby and Horace tucking into one of Fred's scrumptious berry pies, piping hot from the oven.

Who doesn't love pies? he thought sorrowfully. The words lingered in his mind. *Whoooo doesn't love pies ...?*

With a strange calming clarity, a plan began forming in his head – a fusion of memories and half-truths. It didn't involve arguing and it didn't involve fighting; it involved playing along. Whisker refocused on the three owls and tried to contain his excitement.

'It's such a shame, really,' he began.

'What's a shame?' the mother owl asked suspiciously.

'It's a shame you've only got one measly rat for breakfast, when you could be feasting on a delicious rat pie,' Whisker replied.

The owls turned their heads to each other in puzzlement.

'W-what's rat pie?' Houston asked, intrigued.

'What indeed!' Whisker exclaimed. 'Rat pie is the most scrumptious, mouth-watering and delicious dish you'll ever taste! It's succulent, juicy, tender and makes even the toughest of rat tails melt in your mouth.' He paused and continued with a grin, 'But being wise and worldly owls, I expect you already knew that.'

'Oh yes!' the father owl hooted. 'Of course we know about rat pie. Whoooo doesn't? We adore the stuff ... can't get enough ...'

Whisker sighed. 'It's a terrible shame you won't get to taste any today. As you know, rat pie is extremely easy to make, but unfortunately you're missing a key ingredient.'

The owls blinked in disappointment.

'Which ingredient exactly?' the mother owl enquired. 'I mean, I know them all of course, but there are so many variations toooo the recipe ...'

'Endless variations,' Whisker said, going along with her. 'But to bring out the full flavour of the rat you'll need a juicy brown onion.'

'An onion?' she repeated.

'Why of course!' Whisker exclaimed. 'You can't have rat pie without the onion. It would be an outrage!'

The father owl flapped his wings in agitation.

'Owls doooo things according toooo tradition,' he said sternly. 'We have a respectable reputation toooo uphold. If we need an onion, we'll get an onion!'

Whisker tried not to smile.

'A wise decision,' he concurred. 'Onions make all the difference. I, err ... did see some growing down near the river, if you're interested, but I suspect the Hermit will pick them as soon as the sun comes up.'

'The Hermit!' the father owl hooted in disgust. 'We hate the Hermit!'

'We loathe him!' Houston added.

'We despise him!' the mother snapped. 'Don't get me started. He's the rudest rat on the island. Whoooo does he think he is? Always running away and hiding under a rock whenever we try to catch him. Disgraceful!'

The owls glared angrily at Whisker, expecting a response.

'Hear, hear,' Whisker muttered awkwardly. 'He's an

abomination. And he smells!'

'That settles it!' the mother owl shrieked. 'I'll show him whoooo owns the onions!' She beat her wings rapidly and her body rose into the air. 'I'll be back soooon, boys,' she hooted, 'with the biggest, tastiest onion on the island …'

Her voice drifted away in the wind. The two remaining owls stared down at Whisker.

'A little tenderising never went astray,' Houston hooted, prodding Whisker in the stomach with his talons.

'Speaking – of tenderising,' Whisker spluttered between prods, 'I almost – forgot – to mention – the gravy.'

Houston removed his talon and tilted his head to one side. 'Gravy?'

Whisker clutched his chest and took a few calming breaths.

'Well?' the father asked impatiently.

'Every – gourmet pie – has gravy,' Whisker gasped. 'Rich, thick, peppery gravy. Rat rump is far too dry for distinguished owls like yourselves, but with a dash of gravy it's softer than a slug and more tender than a trout.'

'Where does this *gravy* grow?' the father enquired.

'Gravy doesn't grow,' Whisker said. 'It comes in small barrels. I know for a fact there are several barrels of the scrumptious substance bobbing around in the lagoon right now. They tumbled overboard a couple of days ago. You might have seen them roll off my ship?'

'We saw them alright,' the father hooted, 'from a distance, mind yoooou. We refooooose to go anywhere near the lagoooon.'

'It's those slippery fish,' Houston elaborated. 'We hate them nearly as much as we hate that pesky Hermit! They taste far toooo salty and we always get our feathers wet trying toooo catch them.'

Whisker sighed. 'It's for the best, you know. A tiny gravy barrel is far too heavy for any owl to lift. Besides, the barrels have probably broken on the rocks by now.' He shrugged. 'Oh well. At least the fish will be enjoying a delicious gravy treat.'

The father owl puffed himself up again.

'There's no way I'm sharing a drop of *my* gravy with those slimy sea dwellers!' he hooted. 'I'm the lord of this island!' With a flurry of feathers he took off into the sky.

A small smile crept across Whisker's face.

Houston glared down at him, suspiciously. 'I know what you're up toooo, little rat. I've seen your type before. You may have my parents bamboooozled but yoooou don't fooool me one bit.'

'Up to?' Whisker gasped. 'Me? H-how could I possibly be up to anything? I-I'm just lying here at the bottom of the nest …'

'Exactly!' Houston snapped. 'You're loafing around on your lazy behind while the rest of us doooo all the work. It's the height of rudeness yoooou know.' He crossed his wings and hooted in disgust. 'Don't expect me toooo share a single crumb of my delicious rat pie with yoooou!'

'Rat stew you mean,' Whisker corrected.

'Steoooow?' Houston squawked.

'Rat stew,' Whisker repeated. 'You know, tender pieces of rat and onion in a rich gravy sauce.'

Houston was dumbfounded.

'Rat steoooow, oooogh!' he hooted. 'I thought we were having rat pie.'

'Oh no,' Whisker said. 'It's definitely rat stew. You can't have rat pie without the crisp, golden pastry.'

'Pastry?' Houston exclaimed. 'No one said anything about pastry!'

'Really?' Whisker said in surprise. 'I'm sure I mentioned pastry. It's practically all I think about. I love pastry so much I built the entire hull of my ship out of the stuff. It's no wonder the giant eel attacked us. Pastry is to die for! It has the flavour of buttery toast and the crunch of snail shells, without the gritty bits.'

Drool dribbled from the sides of Houston's beak.

'I do hope my ship is alright,' Whisker continued. 'We lost dozens of pastry sheets on the rocks. Most of them washed up on the beach. I suspect the hermit crabs will make their own seaweed pies when the sun comes up ...'

'Hermit crabs!' Houston exclaimed. 'I hate hermit crabs more than I hate the Hermit! Those sneaky cheats are always hiding in their shells and I can never get them out.'

'How terribly selfish of them!' Whisker cried in outrage. 'It would be such an injustice if they got *all* the pastry. I'm more than happy to pitch in and steal a couple of sheets for you – one for the top and one for the bottom. To quote a famous pastry chef: *the provider of the pastry gets the biggest slice of pie!*'

Houston sucked up his drool.

'I'll be the one toooo retrieve the pastry,' he said, stretching his wings. 'That humungous slice of pie is mine!'

He released his grip on Whisker and, with a hoot, he was gone.

Without an owl in sight, Whisker clapped his paws together and stared triumphantly up at the stars.

He couldn't help but start a little victory rhyme:

Twinkle twinkle little star,
rats are wiser, yes we are!
Up above a tree so high,
owls won't put me in rat pie.
Twinkle twinkle little star,
rats are smarter, yes we are!

He finished his tune and lazily sat up.

'Now for the escape,' he said, chuckling to himself. 'Piece of cake ... or should I say *piece of pie!*'

He stuck his head out the top of the nest – and gasped. For the first time he saw exactly where he was. He wasn't at the top of a pine tree as he had thought; he was on a ledge, halfway up an enormous cliff. The huge rocks of the cliff face were as smooth as glass. There was no way up and no way down.

Whisker pounded his fists on the nest, in confounded frustration. He'd been the fool all along.

EIGHT

Pride comes before a ...

A faint glow spread across the eastern sky. On any average day, Whisker would have marvelled at the changing hues of the heavens and stared dreamily at the orange-rimmed clouds of a world waking from its slumber. Dawn made him feel alive, invigorated. But today, the prospect of a glorious sunrise brought him no comfort. He was stuck on a cliff, about to become the main ingredient in a dish he'd foolishly orchestrated. Not even the warm rays of sunlight could thaw his icy disposition.

He crawled out of the nest and shuffled to the edge of the rocky ledge. The wind roared up the side of the cliff from the pine forest far below. Whisker knew he was too high to even consider jumping.

Accepting defeat, he retreated from the edge and gave the nest several hard kicks in anger. It was tightly woven but extremely light and slid across the rock with every kick, the wind buffeting its outer twigs as it moved closer to the edge. Whisker had a sudden urge to kick the nest straight over the side of the cliff.

Serves them right, he thought vindictively. *They'll have to build a new nest out of rat pie!*

He gave the nest several more kicks, imagining the

three owls were sitting in a soggy pool of gravy while their soft nest blew away in the wind … *of course!*

Whisker stopped himself mid-kick. Suddenly the nest had a whole new purpose. He grabbed the closest twigs with both paws and yanked the circular object away from the edge.

Perfect size, he thought, examining it closely. *But it needs a slight modification.*

He squatted down next to the nest and gripped its underside with his fingers. Using the strength of his legs, he slowly stood up, lifting the sides higher and higher into the air until the entire nest was standing upright.

Whisker gave it one last push and the nest dropped upside-down onto the ledge. Wasting no time, he squeezed his body into the hollow cavity at its centre. The nest arched over his head like an igloo, or, as Whisker imagined, a makeshift parachute.

After checking the map and his sword were secure in his belt, he gripped the inner sides of the nest with his paws and wrapped his tail around the twigs behind him. One step at a time, he began dragging it towards the edge.

He felt a gust of wind as the front of the nest slid over the side of the rock. His tail trembled in anticipation and his legs stopped moving as panic set in – he had to be sure he was making the right move. Once he stepped off the cliff, there was no going back.

A distant hoot gave Whisker the motivation he needed. With a jolt of panic, he took the leap of his life and threw himself over the edge.

Like a turtle tumbling through a tornado, Whisker and his shell of sticks plummeted down. The icy wind blasted his face and stung his eyes. Helplessly, he struggled to hold on as the nest flapped from side to side and began to spin. He dug his toes into the nest to steady himself, but he was dropping too fast.

Suddenly, the tops of the tallest pine trees were everywhere and the ground was rushing towards him. Pine needles brushed his tail. He saw a branch in his path and leapt free, wrapping his arms around a prickly pinecone.

The branch bent under his weight, dragging Whisker down. He held on with all his might as the branch sprang up, vibrating back and forth like the string of a harp before finally quivering to a stop.

Nervously, he loosened his grip and looked down. He was only metres from the ground. The nest lay in tatters below him.

'Perfect landing,' he muttered. 'One day I'll get an easy escape.'

He carefully lowered himself from branch to branch and dropped onto a thick bed of pine needles. Relieved to be on solid ground, he looked up at the monstrous cliff, towering high above him. Silhouetted against the pale blue of the dawn sky he saw three owls, flying in a line. The first carried an onion in its claws, the second clutched a small barrel of gravy and the third hauled two broken deck boards.

Crunchy onion pie for breakfast –, Whisker mused. He stopped himself short. *I've already had my own slice of humble pie.*

Sighing to himself, he tightened his belt and set off in the direction of the rising sun.

Somewhere in the middle of the dense forest, Whisker heard a croaky *'HOOT HOOT,'* followed by the overpowering aroma of onion.

He drew his sword and crept forward. The owls had either choked on a piece of onion pie and were out for revenge or an imposter was lurking in the woods.

'Hermit said it was Whisker,' laughed a familiar voice above him.

Whisker looked up. The Hermit and the Captain were sitting on a branch of a tree, clutching small pinecones in each paw like two cheeky children waiting to attack.

Whisker gave them a wave with his sword and the Captain lowered his pinecones.

'You win, Hermit,' the Captain said begrudgingly. 'It's Whisker alright. But I'm certain I smelt owls!'

The Hermit pointed to a feather sticking out of Whisker's shirt.

'That would explain the *fowl* smell,' the Captain joked. 'Fell into a pile of feathers did we?'

'My evening wasn't exactly a *hoot* ...' Whisker replied evasively.

'Well, it's good to find you safe and sound,' the Captain said warmly. 'We were beginning to get a little worried. There are all sorts of nasty creatures out here.' He glanced around warily. 'Owls and scorpions are just the beginning ... I'd hate to think what would have happened if any of them had caught you.'

'L-lucky me, eh?' Whisker stammered, deciding to leave it at that. Being captured by scorpions *and* owls on one night wasn't exactly bragging material.

'Hermit takes Whisker to his rowboat now,' the Hermit said, climbing down from the tree. 'Vessel hidden in dunes.' He threw Whisker a ripe pinecone. 'Whisker hungry, yes, yes?'

'Yeah, thanks,' Whisker replied. 'I'm famished from … err, getting lost – and stuff.'

He hurriedly picked the small nuts from the pinecone and stuffed them into his mouth. At least with his mouth full he couldn't say anything incriminating.

While the Captain collected several more pinecones for their breakfast, the Hermit casually wandered over to Whisker. He glanced at Whisker's torn shorts and grinned.

'Whisker fell into bramble bush *and* pile of feathers, did he?'

Whisker stared back at him with bulging cheeks. 'Mmm- hmm.'

The Hermit gave Whisker a sly look that said *your secret is safe with me* and gestured for Whisker to follow him through the trees. Whisker stuck to the Hermit like a piece of gum clinging to the sole of a shoe. There was no way he was losing sight of him a second time.

The three rats reached a rocky lookout on the outskirts of the forest. The wind, for once, was surprisingly calm. Whisker stood and admired the striking panorama around him. The Rock of Hope lay to the south-east, the waves gently lapping its smooth base – the tide was fully in. Beyond the sandy shore, the curving cliffs of the island surrounded the peaceful lagoon. It was a stark contrast to the Treacherous Sea Whisker had experienced two days ago. The black shapes of the rocks dotted the still, turquoise water like chess pieces on a glassy board.

Whisker caught a glimpse of something silver disappear behind a distant island.

'Down! Now!' the Hermit hissed, pulling Whisker to the ground.

Whisker hit the earth with a hard *THUD* and the Captain dropped beside him. Even with his nose squashed into the dirt, Whisker could see enough to know what was out there. A slender ship appeared in the middle of the lagoon, its silver hull shimmering in the sunshine. Its three square sails flapped gently in the breeze, each emblazoned with a fish skeleton. The ship was too distant for Whisker to identify its crew, but he'd seen that dreaded vessel often enough to know that six of his least favourite felines were onboard.

'Not the rescue party we were hoping for,' the Captain muttered.

Whisker didn't respond. He simply watched in growing dread as the armour-plated vessel of the Cat Fish, the *Silver Sardine,* sailed through the tight passage into the centre of the lagoon.

NINE

On the Prowl

T*he Owl and the Pussy Cat* was Whisker's least favourite nursery rhyme. After narrowly escaping from *owls*, he was not looking forward to adding *pussy cats* to the mix.

The Captain was equally unimpressed.

'Infuriating Cat Fish!' he growled. 'Why do they get the easy run? Fine weather, high tide and not an eel in sight!'

'Cat Fish?' the Hermit gasped. 'Hermit not fond of Cat Fish.'

'No one's fond of Cat Fish,' the Captain muttered. He hesitated and looked directly at the Hermit. 'I should have mentioned this earlier, Father, but we have a particularly nasty crew of cats on our tails and they're as eager as we are to get their paws on the treasure.'

The Hermit twitched his ears nervously. Whisker's tail followed suit.

The Captain continued gravely, 'It was my hope that General Thunderclaw sent Captain Sabre and his feline followers to a watery grave, following an impromptu fireworks show a few nights ago, but the evidence clearly suggests otherwise …'

THE
SILVER
SARDINE

'H-hermit puts key-diving expedition on hold,' the Hermit stammered.

'Obviously,' the Captain grunted. 'Sabre won't be leaving in a hurry. Not without the treasure.'

Whisker felt a wave of panic sweep across his body. The Cat Fish clearly knew what path to take across the lagoon.

What else do they know? he wondered. *Has Sabre solved the mystery of the riddle?*

'W-what's our next move?' he asked in a trembling voice.

'We watch from a distance,' the Captain replied. 'It shouldn't be hard to discover what the Cat Fish are up to.'

'But they'll know we're here!' Whisker shot back. 'They'll see the broken boards on the beach and find the fresh holes at the treasure site.'

'That could work in our favour,' the Captain said thoughtfully. 'If we stay out of sight, the Cat Fish may be fooled into believing we've already dug up the treasure and departed the island. With no treasure to plunder, they'll be gone before the next high tide. This place is hardly a holiday destination.'

'No, no,' the Hermit said in a worried tone. 'If Cat Fish leave, rats will be stranded on windy, windy island forever.'

The Captain shook his head. 'My crew will come back for us. It's only a matter of time. Mark my words.'

The Hermit looked doubtful. 'What if Pie Rats believe Captain and Whisker are dead?'

'That won't stop them searching,' the Captain said defensively. 'They're Pie Rats – loyal to the very end. Why is that so hard for you to see?'

The Hermit stared into the distance. 'Hermit sees what Hermit sees. Hermit sees only silver ship. Maybe …?'

'You can't be serious!' the Captain gasped. 'There's no

way I'm begging for a lift or stowing away on that mobile seafood cannery.'

'No, no!' the Hermit exclaimed. 'Hermit has better idea. Hermit and rats *steal* ship while cats search mountain.'

The Captain glared at the Hermit. 'I'm not leaving the Cat Fish alone on this island – not with the treasure still out there. Who knows what terrible havoc they could wreak with it in their possession?' He paused and then added, 'And I'm definitely not leaving without my crew!'

The Hermit turned to Whisker for support. Whisker was torn between his loyalty to the Captain and his overpowering feeling of guilt. He knew the Hermit had waited years to escape the island. Whisker wondered if he could deny him his one shot at freedom, all for the sake of an unknown treasure they were yet to discover.

For all his noble intentions, however, Whisker knew that as soon as he left the island he would turn around and sail straight back again. He had no doubt the Captain would do the same. Neither of them could spend a life of freedom on a stolen ship, wondering what could have been.

He weighed up his options. The Captain believed the Pie Rats would return and rescue them. If he was right, the Hermit would have his freedom. If he was wrong, they still had the treasure to help them.

Whisker chose to trust his captain.

'I'm sorry,' he said to the Hermit. 'I have a duty to the *Apple Pie*.'

Whisker expected the Hermit to be angry with him, or at least disappointed. But the old rat simply smiled back.

'Hermit wishes crew of *Princess Pie* were as faithful as Whisker,' he said nostalgically. '*Loyalty before all else, even pies* ... Hermit forgets there is more to life than survival.'

He put one paw on Whisker's shoulder and the other on the Captain's arm. 'Hermit is agreed. We all stay. Mashed potato pies will have to wait!'

The Captain laughed heartily and Whisker felt proud to be in the presence of two great captains. Both were as stubborn as oxen, but both were willing to sacrifice all they had for the greater good. Whisker hoped that one day he would be a leader like that.

The three rats crept back into the forest and began their game of *cat and mouse*; or, to be more precise, *six cats and three invisible rats.*

The Hermit led Whisker and the Captain through the trees to the lower outskirts of the western forest, where they could get a closer view of the lagoon. Silently and stealthily, the three rats climbed the upper branches of a tall pine tree overlooking the beach. From their high vantage point, they watched the small party of cats travel to shore in a heavily laden rowboat.

Captain Sabre, the black and orange Bengal, sat at the bow of the boat, his head darting from side to side, searching the dunes for signs of life.

Whisker was well camouflaged in the dense foliage of the tree, but it didn't stop him freezing to the spot like a petrified pigeon. He'd given Sabre a boat load of reasons to want him in a cooking pot and, without wings, Whisker knew the top of a tree wasn't the safest place to be discovered.

The boat landed near the Rock of Hope and Sabre stepped onto the sand. He was followed by Furious Fur, the wild, white Persian, and Master Meow, the glass-eyed silver tabby. All three cats carried large cheese knives, strapped to their backs with thick belts.

Sabre drew his knife and began sharpening its blade on the Rock of Hope, while the others unloaded a cargo of canvas tents, fishing lines and shovels. After two large chests were dragged onto the beach, Master Meow gave Sabre a high-pitched whistle.

Sabre tipped his orange captain's hat to his second-in-command and continued sharpening. Meow climbed into the boat and began rowing back to the *Silver Sardine*.

Furious Fur approached Sabre. Although Whisker couldn't make out the words over the rustling wind in the trees, he saw Sabre pointing to Mt Mobziw and drawing fish shapes in the sand. Sabre's intentions were blatantly obvious: set up camp, catch half-a-lagoon of fish and then dig up the treasure.

Under Sabre's direction, Furious Fur lugged armfuls of canvas and rope to the foot of the dunes. Using long pieces of driftwood for framework, he constructed a primitive-looking shelter. Soon after completion, the rowboat returned with two more passengers.

The '*ladies*' of the crew, Cleopatra and Siamese Sally, pranced up the beach on all fours. Cleopatra, the graceful Abyssinian, gazed straight ahead with hypnotic green eyes. Siamese Sally, bony and bored, looked even more lifeless than usual. Her huge hook-earrings weighed down her scraggly ears. Her red bandanna hung loosely from her skull-like head and a scrap of red material was tied around her scrawny left arm.

A bandage from the fireworks incident, Whisker thought. *Yet another reason for the Cat Fish to have me for lunch.*

He counted the cats. *One, two, three, four, five –*

There was still one crew member missing: Prowler, the Russian Blue and shadowy lookout of the Cat Fish.

Siamese Sally

Captain Sabre

Cleopatra

Master Meow

THE CAT FISH

Furious Fur

Prowler

Whisker turned his gaze to the *Silver Sardine*. He ran his eyes across the deck and then raised them to the broadsword-shaped masts. Something grey and furry moved in the crow's-nest – *Six*.

'I believe we've seen enough,' the Captain whispered. 'There are safer places I'd rather be when the Cat Fish venture inland.'

Without protest, the rats crept down from the tree and set off towards the Hermit's cave on Mt Moochup. The forest thinned as the terrain grew steeper and the three companions found themselves wading through the shallow water of the mountain spring, far upstream from the Rock of Hope.

Whisker stopped and gulped down huge mouthfuls of the crystal-clear water. He hadn't drunk anything for nearly two days, and the water was soothing on his dry throat. His mother once told him that rats could go without water for longer than camels. Whisker thought the spring water could keep him going for weeks, such was its pure taste.

'Whisker needs to keep moving,' the Hermit said from the opposite bank.

Whisker wiped his mouth with the back of his paw and hurried out of the stream, following the Hermit into rocky country. He kept a keen eye out for his black-shelled buddies, the scorpions, and was relieved to reach the Hermit's lair without a repeat of the previous night's desperate dash. If the scorpions were lurking nearby, they were in no hurry to reveal themselves in the light of day.

The Hermit stashed his small bag in its hiding spot at the back of the cave and the three companions took turns monitoring the cats from a nearby boulder-top. It had a clear view of the beach but was too high up the mountainside for the rats to see much more than a few blurs of fur without magnification. The rats took no chances and lay perfectly still on the rock on the off chance the Cat Fish were looking back up at them – with a telescope.

The cats devoted their entire morning to fishing. Whisker thought it a rather odd activity to choose, considering there was a mysterious treasure waiting to be discovered, but he knew it was pointless trying to fathom the logic of cats.

The afternoon brought strong winds and a fierce storm. The rats saw nothing through the pelting rain and quickly abandoned their lookout post, agreeing that the Cat Fish were unlikely to start their treasure hunt in such soggy conditions. Sitting in the corner of the warm cave, Whisker was glad he had solid rock over his head and not the flimsy roof of a canvas tent.

Throughout the wet afternoon, the Captain and the Hermit discussed life back home while Whisker re-examined the Forgotten Map. After hours of analysing, pondering and speculating, all he discovered was one trivial fact: the pine forests had expanded since the map was made.

By boiled onion time, Whisker was thoroughly convinced he could discover no more without the key. As frustrated as he felt, munching on his soggy onion, Whisker knew that Sabre's chances of finding the treasure were even slimmer than his.

The rain continued throughout the night. When the storm finally lifted, before dawn, a thick fog had rolled in.

The rats ventured from the cave to find the entire island shrouded in white. The morning sun, hidden behind layers of dense cloud, failed to warm the cold, damp air. Hazy shapes of boulders rose from the eerie mist like cardboard cut-outs, flat and lifeless.

'Not exactly spying weather,' Whisker said, climbing to the top of a boulder.

'Mist will lift by afternoon,' the Hermit reassured him. 'Eastern trade wind always blows mist away, whoosh, whoosh.'

Whisker extended his paw in front of him. It disappeared into a fluffy white cloud.

'You'd need more than a bit of wind to shift this stuff!' he exclaimed. 'It's thicker than cotton wool.'

'Shh,' the Hermit hissed. 'Voices carry through mist. Whisper only.'

'Sorry,' Whisker whispered.

The three rats spent the misty morning whispering. As the Hermit predicted, a stiff eastern breeze hit the island mid-afternoon, sweeping the blanket of fog out to sea. Whisker and the Captain returned to the boulder to check on the Cat Fish, while the Hermit set off to collect brown onions.

Whisker slid his body to the edge of the rock and peered down. There was no movement from the tent, no activity on the beach, and no sign of the spades the Cat Fish had brought with them.

'They must be out treasure hunting,' Whisker said in a hushed voice.

'It's a possibility ...' the Captain said, his voice trailing off. 'But something doesn't feel right.'

Whisker looked again. The *Silver Sardine* lay anchored offshore, the campsite appeared utterly deserted and the rowboat sat halfway up the beach – on the opposite side of the Rock of Hope.

'That's strange,' Whisker pondered. 'The boat was closer to their camp yesterday.'

'Maybe they went back to the *Sardine* for something,' the Captain whispered.

'Mayb …' Whisker began. He saw a flicker of movement out of the corner of his eye and cut himself short.

He tilted his head to get a better look and felt a jolt of terror convulse through his tail. The cats weren't down at the beach or climbing the opposite mountain; they were directly below him.

The Captain's eye grew wide. Whisker's eyes grew wider.

The rats remained motionless, not daring to move as one by one, Cleopatra, Siamese Sally and Master Meow emerged from a line of bushes and made their way along the rocks.

The three cats moved swiftly and silently, sniffing the air as they went. They weren't hunting for treasure; they were hunting for prey. Whisker cursed the onion he ate for lunch and hoped the cats had colds.

Sally stopped at the foot of the boulder and peered around suspiciously. Whisker held his breath and waited for her to look up. The howling wind was his saving grace. A mighty gust roared over the rocks, carrying the oniony scent of the rats higher up the mountain. Whisker's nostrils were filled with the fishy aroma of the cats below.

Satisfied there was no one about, Sally followed her

companions past the boulder. Whisker continued to stare down at her, afraid to even blink. The handle of Sally's cheese knife clinked on her right earring as she walked. The red bandage on her left arm glided back and forth with every step.

From close range, Whisker could see it was more than just a scrap of material. It had a distinctive shape – a shape Whisker had seen many times before.

With a terrifying realisation, Whisker felt a stab of pain pierce his heart. He stared in disbelief, unable to look away.

Sally's arm band was Ruby's crimson eye patch.

TEN

Despair

Siamese Sally disappeared behind a rock. Whisker's hope disappeared with her. He knew the sight of the crimson patch could mean only one thing: Ruby wasn't coming back.

Stunned, shocked and speechless, he struggled to breathe as a dark cloud of despair engulfed every part of him. He remembered Ruby's terrible secret. Her eye patch was her mask. She never took it off. It covered her past – a past that robbed her of her family and left her blind. It was a cruel reminder of how life could be stolen away. Now Ruby was gone too …

Whisker barely registered the Captain whispering his name or gently shaking his arm. All he could focus on was Ruby: fearless, brave, determined Ruby – the girl who had taught him how to fight, the girl who'd let down her guard and let him into her world.

Ruby was unlike anyone he'd ever met – complex and mysterious. There was so much he never got to say to her. So much he would like to have said. So much he would never find out.

He wished he was still on the ship, fighting beside her.

Could I have saved her? he thought. *Could I have saved*

any of them?

Despairing images filled his head. *If Ruby was gone then Horace, Fred and the others were gone, too. Pie Rats always stick together ...*

'Whisker!' the Captain hissed. 'Whisker!'

Whisker's mind jolted back to the island. The Captain crouched next to him, his finger running over his own eye patch. The pained expression in his eye told Whisker the words he couldn't say.

'T-they're not coming back for us,' Whisker stammered. 'Are they?'

The Captain was silent for a moment.

'Perhaps Ruby's patch was washed overboard when the eel attacked,' he began, 'The Cat Fish went fishing yesterday and –' he stopped himself.

Whisker knew why: Sally was already wearing the armband when the Cat Fish arrived.

The Captain gave up trying to convince Whisker of anything – the Cat Fish took no prisoners and they showed no mercy.

Regardless of how miserable he felt, it was obvious to Whisker that the Captain was hurting as much as he was. Ruby was like a daughter to him. He may have found his father on the island, but his beloved Ruby had been taken away.

The cruel injustice of it all sent Whisker's emotions into overdrive. His eyes burned with tears but his rage burned stronger. Filled with an unholy determination, he set his jaw and drew his sword. His own survival meant nothing to him. All he cared about was revenge.

He crawled to his knees, his anger building, but before he could get to his feet, the Captain grabbed his arm.

'Don't do this!' he pleaded. 'I'm begging you.'

Whisker pulled away.

'I'm not afraid of them,' he said defiantly. 'I've fought them before.'

'It won't bring her back,' the Captain quavered.

'I don't care!' Whisker shouted. 'I don't care! I DON'T CARE!'

The Captain leapt to his feet and seized Whisker by the collar.

'You *do* care!' he hissed. 'And so do I.' He tightened his grip on Whisker's shirt. His eye locked on the young apprentice's startled face. 'You're not going anywhere. Do you hear? That's an order. I'm not about to lose a daughter *and* a son.'

'S-son …' Whisker stammered.

The Captain stared at Whisker, his lips trembling as he spoke. 'I made a pledge to protect you, Whisker. I promised to look after you like you were my own flesh and blood. So far I've failed in my duty and I've put you in harm's way more times than I can count. But this is an island for second chances, not for throwing life away. You're the only crewman I've got now, Whisker, and I need you to be strong – strong like Ruby.'

The Captain released his grip on Whisker. Whisker slowly let go of his anger and returned his sword to his belt.

Powerful feelings of despair, loss and hatred ached inside of him, but they were nothing compared with the agonising feeling of emptiness that swamped his heart. He was accustomed to *living with pain*, but pain was much harder to bear when he was struggling to find a *reason for living*. Inside he was dead, but outside he had to go on.

He wiped his eyes and tried to put on a brave face.

'What now?' he asked feebly.

'First we find the Hermit,' the Captain whispered, 'then we steal the *Silver Sardine* and sail out of here. The Cat Fish can have their cursed treasure.'

Whisker nodded. The map and the key had brought him nothing but misery. It was time he accepted the fact that the treasure would undoubtedly bring him more of the same.

'We must hurry,' the Captain said, 'It's only a matter of time before the Cat Fish return to their camp ...'

'Oh, I wouldn't worry about that,' sneered an evil voice behind them.

Whisker spun around. Towering over him was the menacing figure of Captain Sabre. His hazel eyes glared disdainfully at the two rats. Furious Fur stood to his left, Prowler to his right.

Sabre casually continued, 'The Cat Fish have far more important things to do than take an afternoon siesta on the beach, don't we boys?'

Prowler and Fur both laughed.

Whisker felt his blood boiling. His fingers twitched on the handle of his sword.

'Steady on,' the Captain whispered. 'There's a reason we're still alive.'

'Right you are,' Sabre purred maliciously. 'You see, we find ourselves in a little bit of a pickle. It's rather embarrassing, really, but we've come to ask for your help.'

'You'll get no help from us, you heartless hyenas,' Whisker spat. 'You're speaking to the wrong rats!'

Furious Fur hissed in disgust at Whisker's insulting remark.

'Cut out his tongue!' Prowler growled.

'Gentlemen, please!' Sabre sighed, trying to silence the cats. 'Let's not stoop to their undignified level. Captain One Eye and his pesky apprentice clearly got up on the wrong side of their hovel this morning. I'm sure if we explain our unfortunate plight to them; they'll be more than willing to assist.'

'What do you want, Sabre?' the Captain asked gruffly.

Sabre greedily eyed the map canister on Whisker's belt. 'I think that's obvious, don't you? Several nights ago a couple of particularly important items were stolen from me and I would like them returned.'

'You stole them first,' Whisker muttered.

'Yes, well, that's neither here nor there,' Sabre retorted, locking eyes with Whisker. 'The fact of the matter is, you're going to hand over the key and the map or we're going to pluck you like chickens and barbeque your bones on the beach!'

Furious Fur added his support with a hearty snarl. Whisker paid him no attention. He was distracted by a strange tingle in his nose.

He subtly sniffed the air. A strong sent of onion filled his nostrils.

'Why don't you just feed us to the owls,' Whisker ventured boldly. 'It would be far less trouble. Besides, you don't want to stink out your camp with our smelly bones – we both reek of onions.'

'Owls?' Fur grunted. 'Onions? What?'

'Take a look around,' Whisker said, throwing his paws in the air. 'There are owls and onions everywhere.'

There was a muffled hoot from a nearby bush. Startled, the Cat Fish spun around to see a large onion hurtling towards them.

Before Sabre could react, the flying projectile hit him squarely in the nose. He clutched at his face and hissed furiously.

Prowler and Furious Fur tried to draw their cheese knives, but a barrage of brown onions knocked their weapons flying.

In the confusion, Whisker and the Captain seized their opportunity. Whisker threw himself over the side of the boulder and the Captain followed, sliding backwards down the rough face of the rock. They hit the ground running and darted along the rocky path in a frantic bid to escape.

Whisker saw a flash of grey above him and, the next moment, the agile body of the Hermit touched down with silent precision in the centre of the path.

'Hermit wastes good onions on cats!' he puffed, taking the lead. 'Grass soup for supper!'

He gouged his teeth into the skin of his last onion, covering its surface in small holes. Whisker didn't have the breath to ask what he was doing.

The three rats rounded a corner with the hisses of the cats in their ears and felt the full might of the eastern wind blast them head-on.

The Hermit hurled the onion straight ahead and pulled Whisker and the Captain off the path into a thicket of bushes.

The rats lay deathly still as Sabre and his furious companions raced past them, continuing along the path.

'This way,' Prowler hissed, 'I can smell their filthy stench ...'

The sound of the cats faded away and the Captain whispered urgently to the Hermit, 'We've got to get to the beach and steal the *Silver Sardine* – now. It's our last chance of escape.' His voice trembled. 'My crew aren't coming back –'

The Hermit replied with sadness to his voice. 'Hermit knows short cut. Hermit saves rats.'

Pinning his ears back, the Hermit dashed through the bushes, nimbly weaving his way past thorny branches and rotting logs. Whisker and the Captain followed in close pursuit, reaching a steep, pebbly slope.

The Hermit wasted no time in hurling himself onto the fine gravel as if it were nothing more than a child's slippery slide. The others braced themselves for the descent and slid after him.

Rough chunks of rock grazed Whisker's feet, lodging themselves uncomfortably up his trouser legs. The wind blew hard over his left shoulder and he knew he was close to the eastern edge of Mt Moochup.

The slope continued to fall, twisting its way down the mountain. Stinging and sore, Whisker skidded to a halt at a line of jagged rocks. The terrain looked unfamiliar to him, but the scuttling sounds reverberating around the rocks were instantly recognisable.

He froze on the crest of a rock. Below him, an army of scorpions had gathered in the shadows. The shiny black creatures swivelled their bodies in the rats' direction and scurried up the rocks, pincers snapping, tails stabbing.

The rats turned on their heels and ran.

'Hurry!' the Hermit shouted. 'Back up the mountain!'

Whisker's tail thrashed against passing rocks as he scrambled up the ever-shifting slope. It wasn't just the scorpions that sent his tail into a frenzy, it was the thought of the Cat Fish, waiting somewhere up ahead.

The Hermit made a detour halfway up the slope.

'Eastern path,' he panted. 'Rats escape *behind* mountain.'

Whisker could only imagine what dangers lay behind the mountain – the map had been drawn from the front and gave him no clues. All he knew was that they wouldn't find the *Silver Sardine* – their last chance of escape.

The path wound its way around the mountain, zigzagging around a multitude of fallen obstacles. Whisker caught glimpses of the ocean through gaps in the wind-swept trees clinging to the mountainside. Each trunk grew almost horizontal in the relentless wind.

As the rats gained altitude, the scorpions dropped by the wayside, but the Hermit continued his frantic pace. The path levelled off and opened out onto an exposed ledge, overlooking the eastern sea. Whisker hadn't realised just how high up he was. The wind raced up the side of steep cliffs, almost lifting him off his feet. Mighty waves savaged the rocks far below.

There was no time for sightseeing. In an instant, Whisker had plunged back into the cover of trees and was darting around a sharp bend.

The mountain path straightened. Up ahead, two cats casually strolled into view. Cleopatra spied the rats before any of them could react. She fixed her green eyes on Whisker and sprang towards him with Master Meow bounding after her.

With panicked squeaks, the rats twisted their tails around and fled the way they had come. Three rats on two cats was a survivable fight, but Siamese Sally was certainly lurking nearby.

The ledge loomed directly in front of them, but from an

overhanging branch of a beech oak, a scrawny paw swept through the air.

Anticipating the attack, Whisker ducked beneath Sally's blow. She shrieked in rage and dropped onto the track.

Before Whisker could straighten himself, the Hermit's knobbly toes dug into his back and the grey warrior launched himself high into the air. With a perfectly executed roundhouse kick, he struck Sally in the side of the head.

Sally staggered sideways in a daze and the Captain and the Hermit charged past. Whisker resisted the temptation to punch Sally in the nose and instead wrenched the crimson eye patch from her arm. He stuffed the patch into his pocket and darted onto the ledge as the shadow of Cleopatra appeared beside him.

Head down, Whisker sprinted forward, almost colliding with the two rats, standing frozen in the centre of the ledge.

'Hurry!' he shouted.

His companions didn't flinch.

Whisker looked up to see Sabre and his snarling henchmen skulking towards them. For the second time in as many days, he was trapped on a ledge.

The cats slowly advanced, three from either side, with Sally swaying dangerously close to the edge of the cliff. Whisker hoped the howling wind would blow her gaunt body over the edge, taking Cleopatra with her. With a couple of the Cat Fish gone, his chance of escape would rise from *zero* to *slightly better than zero* in an instant.

Master Meow pulled Sally away from the cliff and Whisker's chance of escape dropped to *less than zero*.

'Why must you insist on these games?' Sabre hissed, inching closer to the rats. 'My patience is wearing thin.'

'*Thin* like layers of onion?' the Hermit muttered.

Sabre glared at the Hermit and drew his sword. 'And who might you be?'

The Hermit held his ground but declined to answer.

Sabre snarled in irritation. 'Regardless of who this insolent onion thrower is, he'll be joining his aromatic companions in the cooking pot if I don't see my map and key quick smart.'

'Err, there's one small problem,' Whisker squeaked, hoping the truth would set him free. 'We don't actually have the key.'

Sabre flashed him a look of contempt. 'Do you really think I'm that stupid? I've heard that excuse ten thousand tiresome times before. We both know perfectly well the key is hidden down your trousers or stuffed in One Eye's hat.'

The Captain removed his hat and gave it a good shake. Nothing came out. The Hermit held out his empty paws. His cloak had no pockets and his small bag was still in the cave.

Whisker considered dropping his trousers, but decided against it when the Cat Fish crew drew their cheese knives and took a collective step closer.

The Captain raised his sword in readiness and the Hermit moved his body into a convoluted fighting pose. Whisker wished he was as confident as the Captain and as courageous as the Hermit, but all he could manage was a backwards shuffle to the edge of the cliff.

Fast running out of options, he wrenched the map canister from his belt and held it over the ocean.

'I'm warning you, Sabre,' he said, in his most convincing voice. 'Come any closer and I'll drop it.'

Sabre rolled his eyes.

'You insult me yet again with another of your predictably tiresome moves, young apprentice,' he scoffed. 'And to think, I was beginning to think so highly of you. Oh, well. There's no shame in dying as a talentless hack when you were born a pathetic rat!'

Jeering and hissing, the Cat Fish crept even closer.

'I'm not bluffing!' Whisker cried. 'I swear I'll drop it.'

Sabre shrugged. 'Do it. See if I care. After I finish you off, I'll have my crew row around and pluck your precious map from the sea.'

In terror, Whisker shifted his eyes from the map to the ocean far below. He had one last option. Sea spray and frothing waves blurred the jagged rocks at the foot of the cliff. Breakers rolled in from all directions. It was no good – without a parachute, any thought of jumping seemed ludicrous. The map canister would survive the fall, but not a live rat.

Whisker felt the weight of defeat dragging him down. His friends were gone. His family was gone. The treasure was lost.

… *What am I fighting for?* The question drifted into his mind. Struggling for an answer, he let his eyes hover aimlessly over the ocean. Amid the swirling blues and greens of the turbulent sea, he caught a glimpse of something golden.

He blinked.

It can't be, he thought.

He looked again, in disbelief. There, on the crest of a white-capped wave, was his answer.

Controlling his excitement, he raised his eyes from the ocean and prepared for the performance of his life.

ELEVEN

The Royal Gala

Sabre pointed his sword at Whisker, clearly unsettled by the young rat's change of disposition. 'Don't tell me, you've come up with yet another desperate reason to let you go?'

'Desperate?' Whisker exclaimed, waving his sword wildly over his head. 'I'm not desperate! I'm excited!'

'You're excited to be skewered and grilled?' Siamese Sally asked mockingly.

'NO!' Whisker shouted, his voice echoing off the rocks. 'I'm excited about the *ROYAL GALA!*'

The Captain's jerked his head in Whisker's direction, awaiting an explanation.

Cleopatra narrowed her emerald eyes. 'You're on a deserted island. I hardly think there's a function hall waiting for your conniving corpses.'

Whisker shook his head and continued to shout, 'The *ROYAL GALA'S* not here! It's at my *GRANNY SMITH'S* house! She'll be cooking lots of *RED, DELICIOUS* dishes. And after you six cats release us from this ledge, we're sailing straight there in the Hermit's *TOFFEE* raft.'

The Hermit looked at Whisker, totally confused. The Captain, starting to understand, shuffled backwards, tugging the Hermit's tattered cloak as he went.

'He's gone mad!' Meow laughed, rolling his glass eye in circles. 'The onions have pickled his brain!'

'Rubbish!' Sally hissed, moving closer to Whisker. She studied him suspiciously with lifeless eyes. 'This isn't a court, little rat. Pleading insanity won't save your wretched, rodent neck!'

Whisker shot a glance over his shoulder and tried to remain confident.

'We stand as one, united on this precipice,' he roared. 'You think you have us cornered, but it's not over 'til the *PINK LADY* sings!'

'It's *fat* lady, I think you'll find,' Sabre corrected. 'And I can assure you there are none of those here.'

Cleopatra battered her eyelashes. Sally continued to look skeletally dead. The Hermit, finally getting Whisker's cryptic message, broke from his pose and joined the others at the very edge of the cliff.

'How long do we need?' the Captain whispered, not taking his eye off Sabre.

'Twenty seconds,' Whisker guessed. 'Give or take …'

'I'll handle it from here,' the Captain muttered.

'Sabre!' he bellowed. 'I'll give you to the count of three to lower your cheese knife and retreat, or you'll taste bitter defeat at the hands of my fearless crew.'

The Cat Fish laughed.

'I'd hardly call those sorry sods standing next to you a *crew*!' Sabre scoffed. 'Go on. Count away.'

'ONE!' the Captain counted. 'For the pies that came before us.'

The Cat Fish stepped into striking range.

'TWO! For the pies we have tasted in glory.'

110

The Cat Fish raised their cheese knives.

'THREE! For the pies you are about to taste.'

The three rats dropped to the ground in unison. There was an awkward pause. Whisker peered up, hoping the grand finale was still on its way.

'I take it we don't get any pie?' Sabre sniggered.

The rats' response came as a chorus of mighty *BOOMS* from the ocean far below. Four flying projectiles hurtled from the sea, blasting the Cat Fish backwards and smothering them in sticky red jelly and short-crust pastry.

The three rats kept their noses nestled into the ground as the bombardment of sugary delicacies continued. Sabre and his bewildered crew staggered to their feet but were knocked down by a second and third sea assault.

When the cloud of icing sugar finally settled, the entire Cat Fish crew were left lying on their backs in gelatinous pools of berry-red jelly.

While the Cat Fish experienced the *sweet* taste of defeat, Whisker and his companions scampered across the ledge on all fours, disappearing down a narrow path. The Hermit couldn't resist scraping a large blob of jelly from Furious Fur's hat on his way past.

'Jelly tarts,' the Captain mused, as they raced along the cliff top. 'A little unorthodox for *Pie* Rats, don't you think?'

'Mmm! Hermit loves tarts, yes, yes,' the Hermit mumbled with his mouth full.

'I'm more of an apple pie rat, myself,' the Captain joked. '*Granny Smith, Red Delicious, Pink Lady* … I'll take any variety!' He winked at Whisker.

A broad smile spread across Whisker's face. His favourite pie was right in front of him.

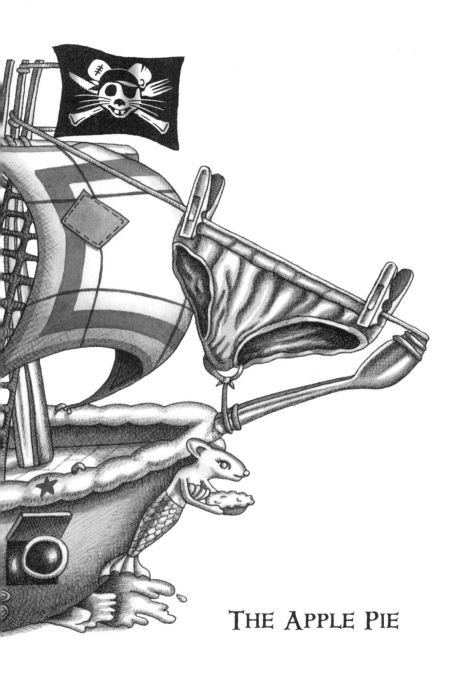

THE APPLE PIE

The good ship *Apple Pie* was sailing along the rocky coast of the island. Her sails were patched. Her deck was repaired. The *Jolly Rat* hung triumphantly from her foremast. To Whisker, the ramshackle vessel was nothing short of magnificent.

Whisker's greatest joy, however, came from the sight of the figure in red prancing across the deck, her unmistakable confidence revealed in every stride.

As Whisker stared, starry-eyed, a pint-sized rat darted from the stairwell, bowling her over in a comical collision.

Ruby and Horace, Whisker sighed. *How I've missed you both …*

The *Apple Pie* turned port side, following the contours of the island and Whisker caught sight of a bright yellow boat bobbing behind her. The Pie Rats had company.

'Is there a way down these cliffs, Father?' the Captain asked.

'Further along,' the Hermit whispered, swallowing the last of his jelly. 'Hermit shows you secret cove, hidden from sight.'

'What about the Cat Fish?' Whisker asked apprehensively. 'Will they come looking for us?'

'It's not likely,' the Captain replied. 'Their ship is unguarded. I doubt they'd gamble their ticket off this island for a wild rat-chase. Still, we'd better keep moving.'

He signalled to the *Apple Pie* with his sword and the much-loved vessel disappeared from sight behind a rocky outcrop of the island. The rats continued south along the edge of the cliffs, slowly making their way to lower ground.

Whisker and his two companions reached the cliffs surrounding the cove at dusk and found Smudge waiting for them. The excited blowfly clutched the branches of a small bush, joyfully buzzing his wings in the wind.

'Friend or foe?' the Hermit asked, eyeing the tiny creature suspiciously.

'Loveable mascot,' the Captain replied.

'He's stronger than he looks,' Whisker said proudly. 'Smudge once kicked the winning goal in a game of Death Ball!'

Smudge raised a small foot in the air as if to say *it's all in the technique.*

The Hermit gave Smudge a nod of approval and began dragging a crudely woven rope from behind a bush.

'One way down,' he chuckled.

Whisker peered over the edge. Steep cliffs curved to either side of him, forming a sheltered cove. There was no sign of the *Apple Pie*. The Hermit tied one end of the rope around the woody stem of a large bush and lowered the other end over the edge.

'*Apple Pie* is anchored beneath rocky overhang,' he said, pointing below. 'Whisker goes first, yes, yes?'

The rope appeared strong enough to support Whisker's weight, and he knew that even if it snapped, he wouldn't have far to fall. He was eager to see his friends and scrambled down the rope with little hesitation.

The *Apple Pie* came into view almost immediately. Whisker saw Emmie and Fred waving to him from the centre of the deck. Pete stood behind the wheel, steering the ship into position. Ruby and Horace crouched on the bulwark, ready to drag him aboard with candy canes, and Eaton and Mr Tribble waited in the shadows of the mainmast.

As Whisker climbed further down the rope he saw two silhouettes in the navigation room – one was tall and slender, the other broad-shouldered and portly.

The *Apple Pie* glided under Whisker and he leapt the last metre onto the ship. He heard the sound of candy canes dropping to the deck, and the next moment, he was in the middle of a five-way hug with Horace, Ruby, Fred and Emmie.

Horace's hook dug into Whisker's ribs, Fred's giant chest almost suffocated him to death and in all the excitement he was certain someone kissed him on the cheek. No one seemed to care that he smelt of onion and the group hug continued for some time.

From the middle of the pack, all Whisker managed to say was a muffled, 'You're alive, you're alive, you're alive!'

'Of course we're alive, *onion* boy,' Ruby said with an endearing grin. We couldn't let you find the treasure without us.'

Whisker looked into her sparkling green eye and tried to find something charming to say. His brain somehow confused *charming* with *stupid*.

'Err, nice flowery eye patch thingy,' he blurted out, regretting the words before they'd left his mouth.

Ruby moved her paw to her hibiscus-patterned eye patch.

'A tacky souvenir from Drumstick Island Retirement Resort,' she confessed. 'It was the only design that came in red.'

'I preferred the skull-and-cross-bones print,' Horace said.

Ruby rolled her eye. 'You're so mainstream, Horace.'

Whisker moved his paw to his pocket, but before he could grab Ruby's crimson eye patch he heard a loud shout from behind him.

He turned to see the Captain drop from the bottom of the rope, fuming with rage. The Captain raised his finger and pointed across the deck.

'What's *he* doing here?' he roared.

Whisker followed the Captain's finger to the navigation room where two figures stood side by side in the twilight. One was Madam Pearl, the wealthy white weasel and fugitive friend of the Pie Rats; the other was Rat Bait, scoundrel, rogue and double-crosser.

Rat Bait   *Madam Pearl*

Reunions

The Captain stormed across the deck, barging past his stunned crew like a rampaging bull.

'You've got a nerve showing up here, Rat Bait!' he shouted. 'After all your lies and deceit, you decide to *weasel* your way onto my ship.' His eyes flashed at Madam Pearl and then back to Rat Bait. 'I know a few cats that would *kill* to have a rat like you aboard their vessel.'

Rat Bait took a step backwards, extending the open palms of his paws in front of him.

'I been meanin' ye no disrespect, Capt'n Black Rat,' he gabbled. 'I can explain everythin'…'

The Captain grabbed Rat Bait by his tattered blue collar and threw him to the deck.

'EXPLAIN?' the Captain roared. 'Explain what? How you deserted your captain, dishonoured his name and then lied to his family?'

Pure terror flashed through Rat Bait's eyes. 'How did ye …?'

'FIND OUT?' the Captain shouted. 'I'll tell you how I found out. I asked a dead rat!'

Rat Bait froze.

A gentle *thud* rippled through the deck. All eyes fixed

on the stranger at the end of the rope.

'It can't be,' Rat Bait choked, turning pale. 'We thought he was gone …'

'You thought WRONG!' the Captain bellowed. 'And now you'll pay for your mistake.' The Captain raised his paw, ready to strike.

'Let him go,' the Hermit said in a soft voice.

'Let him go?' the Captain gasped. 'There's no way I'm letting him go until he gets what he deserves.'

The Hermit moved closer. 'What he *deserves* and what he will *get* are two different things.'

'How can you say that?' the Captain fumed. 'Look what he did to you. He stole your life. He took your freedom. Surely you hate him as much as I do?'

The Hermit looked down at the trembling body of Rat Bait.

'Hate didn't keep Hermit alive on windy, windy island,' he said pensively. 'No, no. Hate blew away in the wind.' He paused. 'Onions kept Hermit alive – Captain gives Rat Bait *onions*.'

'WHAT!' the Captain cried in astonishment. 'Onions? You can't be serious. Can't you see what he is? What he will do?'

'He came to help you, Captain,' Madam Pearl said boldly. 'I know it's not my place but …'

'You're right, it's not your place!' the Captain snapped, turning to Pete for support.

'We had no choice,' Pete said deadpan. 'Rat Bait repaired the *Apple Pie* free of charge. We used the silver plates to purchase the materials, but there was nothing left for the labour.'

'A likely story,' the Captain muttered. 'I suppose he

decided to stay onboard when he heard we'd located the key.'

Rat Bait shook his head but kept his mouth shut.

'We volunteered for the voyage when we heard you went overboard,' Madam Pearl explained. 'I for one had a debt to repay after you rescued me from Prison Island.' She shot Whisker a grateful look.

'And you, Rat Bait?' the Captain growled. 'What's your excuse? Treasure? A reward?'

'G-guilt …' Rat Bait quavered, staring at the Hermit. 'Guilt for past indiscretions.'

There was silence and the Captain slowly lowered his fist. 'I know your type, Rat Bait. I know what you're playing at. When this is all over, we'll see who you really are.' Without a word to his crew, the Captain strode past Rat Bait and stormed down the stairs.

Shell-shocked, the crew stared after him.

'Well, that went well,' Horace muttered.

Whisker didn't know what to say – or what to think. It certainly wasn't the joyous reunion he'd been expecting. Rat Bait was a greedy coward and a first-class liar, granted, but part of Whisker wanted to believe the scoundrel had truly changed his ways. In the end, Whisker decided it was best to act as the gracious rat his mother had taught him to be and helped Rat Bait to his feet.

''Tis a pleasure to see ye again, li'l Whisker,' Rat Bait said, in a shaky voice. 'Lady Luck is still on yer side I see.'

Whisker nodded expressionlessly. Rat Bait took a deep breath and extended his paw to the Hermit. 'For what it's worth, I offer ye me loyalty, Capt'n Ratsputin. I don't expect yer forgiveness. But I'll take yer onions an' do me best to make things right.'

The Hermit stared long and hard at Rat Bait, his ears twitching from left to right as he considered the scoundrel's apology. Finally he spoke in a resolute voice. 'Hermit doubted any of his crew would return. Hermit is glad he was wrong.' He clutched Rat Bait's paw and laughed, 'Onions can wait! Hermit wants potato pies!'

Fred acknowledged the Hermit's request with an affirmative grunt and wandered below to the galley, quickly followed by Mr Tribble. The others crowded around the Hermit. Ruby looked unusually flustered.

Horace nudged Whisker and whispered, 'So that's Ruby's grandfather, right?'

'Uh huh,' Whisker replied.

The Hermit gave Ruby a warm smile and Ruby's face contorted into a pained frown. She buried her head in her paws and sprinted down the stairs. The Hermit stared after her in disappointment.

'Don't take it personally,' Horace said, trying to cheer him up. 'You were the most hated rat on the seven seas until five minutes ago! But don't worry, she'll get over it – she's got Rat Bait to hate now!'

The Hermit looked far from comforted. Rat Bait gave a resigned shrug. Whisker dragged Horace over to the navigation room before he could make things worse. They passed Madam Pearl on their way.

'Hello, Whisker,' she said in an elegant voice. 'Staying alive, I see?'

'Only just,' Whisker replied honestly. 'And you, Madam Pearl?'

'Oh, you know me,' Madam Pearl said with a sly smile. 'Living it up as a black-market antiques dealer-turned-fugitive; bunking down in the basement of Rat Bait's bungalow.' She sighed. 'Still, a musty basement beats a prison cell.'

'You should see all the cool diving gear Madam Pearl brought with her, Whisker!' Horace broke in. 'We were going to dive for your bod –' He cut himself off.

'It was meant as a last resort,' Madam Pearl clarified.

Whisker gulped at the thought.

'Maybe we'll find another use for it?' Horace said.

'Maybe …' Whisker considered, an idea forming in his mind.

Madam Pearl interrupted his thoughts.

'Whisker,' she said hesitantly. 'As I promised, I made a few enquiries about your family.'

Whisker guessed by the tone of her voice that the news wasn't good.

'I'm sorry,' she said. 'No one saw or heard anything.'

'Thanks – anyway,' Whisker mumbled, unable to hide his disappointment.

'On another note …' Madam Pearl began.

She was cut off by a whistle from Rat Bait, eager to introduce her to the Hermit.

'I'll tell you later,' she whispered to Whisker.

Whisker gave her a weary nod and followed Horace into the navigation room. He removed his sword and the map from his belt and laid them on the table. Yawning deeply, he slumped down in a cushioned chair.

'I'm all ears, Horace,' Whisker said. 'Fill me in from the top. Last I remembered you were being towed out to sea by a giant eel.'

'Oh, him,' Horace snorted. 'He was a nasty piece of work. Ugly, for a start, and far too persistent for my liking. We were halfway across the Cyclone Sea before we managed to sever all the ropes – my, err, net was stronger than it looked.'

'Tell me about it,' Whisker muttered. 'So, what happened next?'

'Fred saw the eel disappear in pursuit of a school of herrings. I guess the horrid brute run out of puff and settled for an easy meal. After that, the wind blew us to the south. We had to bail pretty hard to stay afloat, but in the end we reached the harbour of Drumstick Island.'

'Is that when you found Rat Bait?' Whisker asked.

'Not straight away,' Horace explained. 'We went in search of Fred's mates, the hamsters – you can thank them for the jelly tarts. Anyway, they mentioned that a new rat had moved into the retirement resort and Pete had a sneaky suspicion it was Rat Bait. Gossip travels fast in retirement circles and Rat Bait found us before we found him. He told us he'd been harbouring a fugitive from Port Abalilly, Madam Pearl. She made her way to the island after the Blue Claw disbanded their naval blockade.'

Horace lowered his voice. 'Between you and me, I think Rat Bait and Madam Pearl have a soft spot for you, Whisker. The instant they heard you'd dived in to save the Captain, they offered to do whatever they could to find you.'

Whisker wasn't sure if he should feel honoured or embarrassed. It seemed he was making a regular habit of picking up scoundrels for friends.

'So how did you know where to find us on the island?' he asked.

'It was a combination of poor weather, shonky navigation and remarkably good luck!' Horace replied. 'We were racing towards the island when the morning mist closed in. It was near impossible to see where we were going. When the mist finally cleared, we found ourselves way off course to the east. Fortunately, Fred spotted your little performance on the cliff top. We loaded the cannons and waited for the countdown. I know jelly tarts aren't technically pies, but who's complaining?'

'Sabre, for a start,' Whisker laughed. 'I've never seen a captain with so much jelly up his nose! Your shooting was pie-point accurate!'

Horace brushed the comment aside with his hook. 'Argh, don't mention it. It's what friends do, right?'

Whisker nodded. 'Jelly tarts all the way.'

'Speaking of food,' Horace said. 'What's with the onions?'

Whisker sniffed an armpit. 'Oh, the onions! Well, that's a long story ...'

'Go on,' Horace said, eagerly.

Whisker collected his thoughts. 'It all began when yours truly did something rather clumsy and dropped the key over the side of the ship.'

Horace looked puzzled.

'But Ruby ...' he gasped.

'I know, I know,' Whisker said, cutting him off. 'She'll be furious with me!' He reached his paw into his pocket. 'Don't worry, I've got something to calm her down.'

He pulled out Ruby's crimson eye patch.

Horace's jaw dropped. 'W-w-where did you get that?'

'Siamese Sally,' Whisker said casually. 'I'm guessing she found it in the Cyclone Sea – I'm not the only one who drops things overboard!'

Horace's eyes grew larger than pie platters.

'Th-that's impossible,' he spluttered. 'Ruby's eye patch vanished from her room on Drumstick Island.'

Friend or Foe

Horace snatched the eye patch from Whisker's paw and hastily stuffed it under his shirt.

'Not a word to anyone,' he hissed. 'Understand?'

'Of course,' Whisker said, confused. 'But …?'

'I'll explain later,' Horace whispered. 'Bring the map and follow me. There's something you need to see.'

Horace led Whisker down the stairs to Ruby's cabin. They found her door securely locked. Horace glanced suspiciously around the corridor and gave the door a firm knock with his hook.

'Go away!' came a muffled cry from inside.

'Let us in, Ruby,' Horace pleaded. 'We need to talk to you.'

'What about?' Ruby hissed.

Horace looked at Whisker for an answer. Whisker shrugged, clueless as to what was going on.

Horace moved his lips to the key hole and whispered, 'Onions.'

'Is Whisker with you?' Ruby asked, a little more interested.

'Err, yes,' Whisker said, sniffing his second armpit. 'We've got a present for you – don't worry, it's not an onion.'

There was a pause followed by the soft *click* of a key turning in the lock. Horace gave Whisker a hooks-up.

Ruby opened the door and pulled the two rats inside, locking the door behind them. She plonked herself down in a red beanbag and folded her arms.

'Well?' she asked, impatiently.

'Lovely to see you too, Ruby,' Horace muttered, pulling out the crimson eye patch and throwing it into her lap.

Ruby took one look at the eye patch and leapt to her feet.

'You little thief!' she roared. 'I knew it was you all along. Get out of my room before you steal something else!'

She grabbed Horace by the shoulders and marched him towards the door.

'A little help please, Whisker,' Horace squeaked.

Whisker stepped sideways, blocking the door.

'Get out of my way!' Ruby hissed.

'Come on, Ruby,' he pleaded. 'Horace didn't steal your eye patch, I gave it to him.'

Ruby pushed Horace aside and glared at Whisker. 'You're lying! Someone stole that eye patch from my room on Drumstick Island while I was taking a bath, and it couldn't have been you. You were stuck here on *onion* island!'

'They're all valid points,' Horace said, 'But if you just let us explain …'

'I don't want your filthy explanations!' Ruby shouted. 'I want you both out of my room!'

Whisker refused to budge. 'Why don't you smell it?'

'Smell *what*?' Ruby snapped.

'Your eye patch, of course,' Horace chimed in. 'You'll be

un-pleasantly surprised.'

Ruby cautiously moved the eye patch to her nose and took a sniff. She frowned and sniffed again.

'Kitty litter and sardines,' she said, perplexed. She studied the eye patch closely and then hastily pulled it away. 'Oooh, gross! It's covered in cat hair!'

'*Siamese* cat hair to be precise,' Horace clarified.

Ruby shook the eye patch furiously in front of her. 'What's Siamese cat hair doing on my eye patch? Siamese Sally was never in my room.'

'Exactly,' Horace said. 'But someone else was.'

Ruby looked horrified. 'Who?'

Horace shrugged. 'It could have been anyone on this ship. The rooms of the bungalow were all connected and none of the doors had internal locks.'

Ruby sat down in the beanbag and began to pluck cat hair from the eye patch.

'Can I have my apology now?' Horace asked cautiously.

'You're still a suspect,' Ruby muttered. 'Everyone's a suspect – except Whisker, and my uncle.'

'Don't forget the Hermit,' Whisker said. 'I doubt he's been in anyone's room for years.'

Ruby sighed. 'Oh him, the scoundrel who's not a scoundrel ... I should probably talk to him, shouldn't I? I mean, he's my grandfather after all.'

Whisker nodded. 'You'll like him, Ruby.'

Ruby stared straight at Whisker. 'Go on. What is he like?'

'Err, he's a bit wind-swept around the edges,' Whisker replied truthfully, 'but once you get past the onion odour, you'll find he's a top grandfather – not that I know much about grandfathers. My grandfather ran away before my father was even born and I never met my great-grandfather Anso, the famous explorer and story teller ...' Whisker realised he was blabbering – a common occurrence when Ruby was staring at him.

He returned to the topic. 'You should see your grandfather's fighting moves. He's got a sensational roundhouse kick. I think he knows rat-fu or something.'

Ruby smiled. 'I might have to ask him for some fighting tips.'

'Ahem,' Horace interrupted. 'If we're done with the family talk, we still have a small problem: There's potentially a thief on our ship.'

'But why would anyone want to steal my eye patch and give it to the Cat Fish?' Ruby asked.

'To convince us you were dead,' Whisker said coldly. 'And they almost pulled it off. It's a good thing they didn't factor jelly tarts into the equation!'

'But why target *me*?' Ruby said, confused. 'Pete's the second in command.'

'You're forgetting something,' Horace said. 'You're the Captain's niece and Whisker's g – err, *good* friend.'

Both Whisker and Ruby blushed the colour of the eye patch.

Horace continued talking through the awkward moment. 'I think it's time we showed him, Ruby.'

'S-showed me what?' Whisker asked with burning cheeks.

Ruby crept to the far corner of the room and prised a loose board from the wall. She stuck her paw into the cavity and removed a small pink bundle. Whisker recognised it immediately as Ruby's pink Pie Rat flag.

Ruby carefully unfolded the flag to reveal a pink-lipped

Pie Rat skull with a crossed lollypop and candy cane. Beneath the skull lay the King's Key.

Whisker stared in wonder.

'You're not as clumsy as you thought,' Horace said.

'But I saw it fly out of my paws!' Whisker exclaimed.

'But did you see it land?' Ruby asked smugly.

'No,' Whisker replied.

Ruby rolled her eye. 'Typical! Boys are always jumping to conclusions!'

'You can't talk!' Horace shot back. 'You thought *I* stole your eye patch.'

Ruby opened her mouth to retaliate, but Whisker jumped in before a gender war could break out. 'Where did you find the key?'

'It was wedged between two deck boards,' Ruby said. 'I kicked my toe on it while I was helping Rat Bait repair the ship.' She glared at Horace. 'It's not the only thing that deserves a good kick.'

Horace deflected her comment with a flick of his hook.

'So why was the key hidden in the wall?' Whisker asked.

'It's no secret Ruby doesn't trust our new crew members,' Horace explained. 'So we hid the key in the wall and circulated a rumour that it was in your pocket when you went overboard. In light of the eye patch incident, it was probably a wise move.'

'We've suspected Rat Bait's involvement with the Cat Fish for some time,' Ruby said. 'He knows more about the treasure than anyone.'

'But Sabre loathes him,' Whisker argued.

'Exactly!' Ruby said. 'And it makes him the perfect spy. Rat Bait wouldn't think twice about ratting us out to save his own skin, and there's a strong chance he's in cahoots with Madam Pearl. He once gave her the Forgotten Map to look after and she's the type of two-faced weasel who would sell her sister to the Cat Fish!'

'Ruby's right,' Horace said in growing dread. 'The Cat Fish have a nasty habit of showing up at the most opportune moments. They've either got perfect timing or there's a sneaky insider in our crew ...'

Whisker gulped.

'It's not just Pearl and Rat Bait I don't trust,' Ruby whispered, glancing around suspiciously. 'Mr Tribble has been acting pretty strange lately and Pete's convinced he's up to something.'

'Mr Tribble?' Whisker exclaimed. 'No way! He's the

most honest rodent on the ship.'

'You haven't seen him recently,' Horace said grimly. 'He's even more anxious than he used to be. He lurks in the background, listening to everything, but barely speaks a word.'

'He did seem rather aloof when I came aboard,' Whisker recalled. 'He didn't even say hello.'

Horace nodded thoughtfully. 'Cast your mind back to Sea Shanty Island, when the Cat Fish were searching for Whisker. I clearly recall finding Mr Tribble alone in the mapmaking section of Salamander's supply shop. We know Sabre entered the store while Mr Tribble was in there, and there was plenty of time for the two to cut a deal.'

'Isn't that a bit out-of-character for Mr Tribble?' Whisker said.

'It's not as out-of-character as timid Mr Tribble volunteering for every one of our dangerous missions!' Horace retorted.

'Make that every dangerous mission *except* raiding the *Silver Sardine*,' Ruby said. 'It's clear where his allegiance lies.'

As Whisker struggled to separate *fact* from *speculation*, he remembered a strange incident involving Mr Tribble and the Forgotten Map. He didn't want to betray Mr Tribble unjustly, but his friends had a right to know.

'There's something I haven't told you,' Whisker said. 'It happened on the night we visited Port Abalilly. I was with Mr Tribble in the *Portside Boutique* when the manager, Selma, brought out the Forgotten Map. I was eager to lay my paws on the map, but Mr Tribble reached out and snatched it from under my nose. He told me he needed to verify the map before I could bring it back to the ship.

The strange thing was, when he did examine it, he barely unrolled a corner. I'm not sure if this means anything, but I suspect he knew more about the map than we did.'

'Maybe he had a tipoff from the Cat Fish?' Horace pondered. 'There might be a secret marking on the map?'

The three rats paused to consider this new information. Whisker took out the map but couldn't bring himself to unroll it. He felt uncomfortable. It wasn't just the thought of Mr Tribble that worried him: it was the prospect that Rat Bait and Madam Pearl could also be back-stabbing spies. Despite their shortcomings, all three were his friends. He'd fought with them, he'd escaped danger with them and he wanted to believe they were all on his side.

Maybe they had me fooled from the start? he thought.

There was a knock at the door.

'Dinner's ready!' Emmie squeaked. 'Piping hot mashed potato pies. Come and get it!'

Whisker knew the rest of the conversation would have to wait. He returned the map to its canister, while Horace wrapped the key and the eye patch inside the flag. Ruby placed the flag inside the wall and pushed the board back into place.

'I think we should tell the Captain what we know as soon as dinner is over,' she whispered.

Whisker nodded. 'If anyone can make sense of this situation, it's definitely the Captain.'

Anxiously, the three rats crept from the room and Ruby locked the door behind them. In sixteen short steps they were seated at the dinner table with the rest of the crew – traitors and all.

The Sting

D inner was an awkward time of suspicious stares and sideways glances. Pete stared at Mr Tribble. Ruby stared at Madam Pearl. The Captain glared at Rat Bait, while Horace shifted his eyes between Mr Tribble, Rat Bait and Madam Pearl. At the far end of the table, Mr Tribble stared at the floor.

Whisker sat at the *cheery* end of the table next to the hungry Hermit, who devoured slices of mashed potato pie quicker than Fred could serve them. In the end, Fred plonked an entire potato pie in front of him and handed him a spoon. The Hermit used his paws.

The mood lightened considerably when Ruby struck up a conversation with the Hermit about paw to paw combat. Despite Ruby's pristine appearance and the Hermit's dishevelled exterior, the two were remarkably similar. By the end of second helpings, both were standing on their chairs, re-enacting epic escapes from the Hermit's past.

'Dessert will be served shortly!' Emmie squeaked from the doorway of the galley.

The Hermit patted his bulging belly and climbed down from his chair.

'Hermit is stuffed like a turkey and begs to be excused,'

he said, with a small burp. 'Hermit wishes to collect his belongings before he leaves windy, windy island.'

There had been no discussion of leaving the island, nor of staying to find the treasure, but the Hermit was clearly eager to depart.

'I'll come with you,' Ruby volunteered.

The Hermit shook his head. 'Island can be dangerous on moonless nights.' He gave Whisker a knowing look. 'Hermit goes alone ... but maybe with protection.'

'Scissor swords, dynamite, a cannon – take whatever you want,' Horace said generously. 'And if you accidently blow up the *Silver Sardine*, all the better!'

The Hermit left the room chuckling to himself.

Following dessert, the Captain sulked off to his cabin. One by one, Ruby, Horace and Whisker excused themselves from the table and headed for the Captain's quarters. Whisker was the last to arrive.

He entered the luxurious carpeted room, surprised to find Pete sitting at the Captain's ornate desk with the others. Smudge was perched on the clock, watching intently. The secret discussion was already in full swing.

'... Mr Tribble doesn't strike me as a spy,' the Captain whispered, 'even though the evidence goes against him.' He breathed deeply. 'My money's still on Rat Bait. He's the rottenest egg in the henhouse!'

'There's a chance all three of them are involved,' Pete murmured. 'Tribble could be the main spy and others his backup. Ruby's eye patch only disappeared *after* we ran into Madam Pearl and Rat Bait.'

'But how can we be certain?' Horace asked in a hushed voice. 'We can't exactly torture the truth out of them – that's more of a Cat Fish thing to do!'

'There is one tried and true method that doesn't involve torture,' the Captain considered. 'It's what we in the industry like to call *The Sting*. Simply put, it's an elaborate trap with an irresistible bait.'

'What kind of bait?' Horace whispered excitedly. 'Gold-plated pies? Choc-coated cherries …?'

Pete screwed up his nose. 'Not food, you dim-witted dugong. A *map-coated key*!'

The Forgotten Map lay open on the Captain's desk. The King's Key rested beside it. Pete and the Captain leant over the two items, their backs to the open door. Pete tapped his pencil impatiently while the Captain muttered quietly to himself. The happy chants of Fred and Emmie drifted from the galley:

Pecan pies for breakfast,
pumpkin pies for brunch.
If the crew are starving
serve them both for lunch!

There was a crescendo of pots and pans as the verse came to an end. The three rats hiding in Ruby's cabin winced.

'I wish they'd shut up!' Ruby whispered. 'I can't hear anything with that awful screeching in my ears!'

'At least you can *see*,' Horace groaned. 'You get the keyhole while I get the lousy gap under the door. Watching floorboards will hardly catch me a spy!'

'Shh!' Ruby hissed. 'Your whining is worse than Fred's singing.'

Horace flattened his face against the floor and breathed

in a noseful of dust.

Whisker remained silent. He had the best view in the house. Through a large crack in the wall, he could see straight down the corridor and into the Captain's cabin.

The sounds of Fred and Emmie grew softer as their dishwashing turned to dish-drying. The lamp in the corridor flickered out.

Now the real action begins, Whisker thought.

The Captain and Pete raised their voices, speculating on the meaning of the riddle. Whenever something important was discussed, they reverted to soft whispers. To anyone listening, their conversation was both highly intriguing and highly frustrating – exactly as planned.

After a lengthy critique of the map, Pete and the Captain turned their attention to the key.

'Have we considered the shape of the teeth yet?' the Captain asked.

Pete lifted the key off the table and held it in front of him. The Captain moved closer, blocking the key from watching eyes.

'Very interesting,' he said. 'The teeth appear to be symbols. This first one could well be a …'

'Aaachoo!' Pete sneezed, cutting the Captain off.

'Bless you,' the Captain said. He pointed to the key and continued, 'And this one is definitely a letter …'

'Aaachoo! Aaachoo!' Pete sneezed again.

The Captain handed him a handkerchief. 'Do try and keep your nasty germs off our precious key, Pete.'

Pete blew his nose. 'Sorry, Captain. It must be the onion odour in the air, playing havoc with my sinuses.'

The Captain grunted and returned to his investigations.

'Ratbeard's reward!' he marvelled. 'Take a look at this!

The third tooth, turned ninety degrees forms a perfect …'

'Aaachoo! Aaachoo! Aaachoo!'

'Enough!' the Captain snapped. 'I'll never decipher anything with your infuriating outbursts, Pete. It's a healthy dose of *Salamander's Sniffle Solution* for you.'

'Aye, Captain,' Pete muttered. 'But you'd better take some, too. It could be contagious.'

The Captain groaned. 'How inconvenient.'

'Doctor's orders,' Pete sniffled. 'Follow me.'

The Captain plonked the key on the table, blew out the candle and reluctantly followed Pete out of the room. Pete clomped a few steps down the corridor and took a detour into the mess room.

'I think the *Sniffle Solution* is in the pantry,' he murmured. 'I recall seeing it behind the flour jars …'

The door to the mess room swung shut, plunging the corridor into silent darkness. Whisker's tail twinged with anticipation.

Before his eyes had time to adjust, he saw a shadowy figure creep past him, quietly shuffling its feet along the gloomy passageway – it seemed the spy had taken the bait.

The ghostly silhouette stopped at the end of the corridor, glanced both ways and then stepped through the open doorway to the Captain's cabin.

With a frantic *BUZZ* of wings, Smudge dropped from the ceiling and clamped himself onto the intruder's head.

'Now!' Ruby cried, wrenching her door open.

The door collided with Horace's nose and came to an abrupt halt. Horace bit down on his hook to stop himself yelping.

Ruby leapt through the narrow gap and charged into

the darkness. Whisker was right behind her, and reached the Captain's cabin in seconds.

A dark figure staggered from the doorway, frantically waving its arms above its head. Ruby hurled herself at the intruder and the two of them tumbled to the ground.

The corridor suddenly filled with light as Pete and the Captain burst from the mess room, quickly followed by Fred and Emmie. An even brighter light lit up the space when Eaton appeared with his precious lantern. Its narrow beam shone the entire length of the corridor, illuminating the trembling figure on the ground.

Emmie squealed, Eaton gasped and Pete stamped his pencil in triumph. Mr Tribble was sprung.

Ruby rose to her feet and drew both swords. Smudge gave Mr Tribble one last poke in the ear and buzzed up to the rafters. Mr Tribble, still sprawled on his back, continued to tremble.

There was a groan from Ruby's cabin. Horace staggered out, clutching his nose.

'So who done it?' he cried. 'I owe him, or her, a knee to the nose!'

'Trembling Tribble's your mouse,' Pete sneered. 'And a knee to the nose may improve his pathetic poker face.' He prodded Mr Tribble with his pencil leg. 'Should have paid more attention at *spy school*, hey Tribble?'

Emmie rushed forward, her eyes red, but the Captain pulled her back. Eaton watched, frozen to the spot, halfway down the corridor.

'N-n-no,' he stammered in disbelief. 'M-M-Mr Tribble's just a teacher.'

Behind Eaton, Rat Bait and Madam Pearl appeared from the cargo hold, their faces filled with surprise. Madam

Pearl placed a paw on Eaton's shoulder to calm him down. The entire crew awaited an explanation.

'It's not what you think,' Mr Tribble gasped. 'I'm not a spy!'

'Really?' Ruby said, unconvinced. 'You look like you were spying to me.'

Mr Tribble gave Whisker a pleading look. It was the first time he'd made eye contact with Whisker since the rescue, and Whisker could see the desperation in his eyes; along with something else – confusion. Mr Tribble was either a brilliant liar or there was more to the situation than any of them had first realised.

Whisker took a gamble.

'Hear him out,' he said. 'If he doesn't explain himself in three minutes, you can maroon him on the island with the Cat Fish.'

'A generous offer, Whisker,' Pete murmured. 'I would have given him *one*. Alright, Tribble, start talking. Your time starts now!'

Mr Tribble peered up at his hostile captors.

'You have to believe me,' he pleaded. 'I'm on your side.'

'So why did you creep into my cabin?' the Captain growled.

'I just wanted to look at the map and the key,' he replied.

'Why?' Pete snapped. 'So you could steal them?'

'No!' Mr Tribble cried. 'Because I'm responsible!'

'Responsible for what?'

'I can't say.'

'Why can't you say?'

'I can't say because I swore an oath!'

'An oath to the Cat Fish?'

'No! An oath to the Cartographer's Guild.'

'The Cartographer's Guild?'

A wave of confused murmurs swept through the crew.

'I know we've been through this before,' Horace whispered to Whisker, 'but tell me again. Cartographers make *carts*, right?'

'Maps,' Whisker said. 'Cartographers make maps.'

'Right,' Horace acknowledged. 'It all makes perfect sense.'

'Does it?' Whisker said.

'No. Not really,' Horace admitted. 'But there's no denying Mr Tribble likes maps.'

'Time's running out, Tribble!' Pete hissed. 'If you don't spill the beans soon, we'll break more than just a silly oath!'

Mr Tribble gritted his teeth. Emmie began to cry.

'What are you hiding?' Pete yelled. 'Tell me! Why is the map so important to you?'

Mr Tribble finally broke. 'BECAUSE I MADE IT!'

Stunned silence filled the corridor.

'Woah!' Horace gasped. 'I didn't see that coming.'

The Captain stared at Mr Tribble in astonishment. 'So you're telling us that *you* made the Forgotten Map?'

Mr Tribble shook his head. 'Not the original Forgotten Map. Only the copy in your possession.'

'Copy?' Horace echoed. 'Why did you make a copy?'

Mr Tribble raised a trembling paw and pointed to the stairwell. 'Because *he* asked me to.'

FIFTEEN

The Maker of Maps

The Hermit reached the bottom of the stairs. His fur was moist, his cloak was damp. In his paw, he clutched a brown drawstring bag.

'Shiver me stitches!' Horace exclaimed, rubbing his bruised nose with his hook. 'This gets stranger by the minute.'

'It's making my head hurt,' Fred groaned. 'I need a pie and a lie down.'

The Hermit looked around the sea of surprised faces.

'Did Hermit miss something?' he asked.

'You could say that,' Horace replied candidly.

Pete continued to eye Mr Tribble suspiciously. 'Let me get this straight, Tribble, you're telling me that the map lying in the Captain's cabin is a *copy* of the Forgotten Map and you made it for the Hermit?'

'That's right,' Mr Tribble said. 'It was many years ago.'

'Yes, yes!' the Hermit exclaimed, his ears twitching madly. 'Hermit thought Tribble looked familiar. Tribble was apprentice mouse mapmaker!'

'I thought he was a teacher?' Horace said, perplexed.

Pete screwed up his nose. 'Oh my precious paws! We'll be here all night at this rate. Can someone just explain

142

what's going on from beginning to end so we can decide what to do with him?'

Ruby lowered her swords. 'We can't feed him to the Cat Fish for copying a map. That's for sure.'

Mr Tribble gave her a look of relief and began to explain, 'When I was a young mouse, my father owned a cartographer's shop in Two Shillings Cove. I was his apprentice. One day, when my father was out of town on business, a sprightly Pie Rat captain came into the shop and asked me to copy a map in his possession. He needed the work done in a hurry so I worked through the night, replicating every last detail, including the keyhole in the centre.

'When the captain returned the following morning to collect the two maps, I pointed out one slight difference so he knew which map was which. At the bottom right of the original map there were two sets of waves. On the copy there were three.

'Such was the nature of my cartographer's oath that I never asked questions, or spoke of the map with anyone again. My father's business closed down when a big mapmaking chain moved into town and I took my love of maps and became a history teacher. I presumed I would never see the map again.'

'Go on,' Horace encouraged.

Mr Tribble continued, 'Years later, aboard this very ship, I heard rumours that a mysterious map had resurfaced. The description of the map sounded vaguely familiar to me, but it was only after I had examined it in the Portside Boutique that I knew for certain it was the same map I had made. The three sets of waves in the corner were an instant giveaway.'

143

He looked around the corridor at the mesmerised crew. 'Since that discovery, I have gone out of my way to keep you all safe – breaking laws and volunteering for ridiculous missions! As the creator of this map, I'm responsible for the trouble it brings. You can imagine my dismay when Whisker and the Captain were lost in the Treacherous Sea.'

He concluded, 'After the Hermit came aboard I laid low to avoid being recognised – the past is best left in the past.'

Whisker continued to stare at Mr Tribble in bewilderment. He felt like a fool. He guessed the others felt the same way – Mr Tribble was on their side all along.

The Captain reached down and helped Mr Tribble to his feet.

'I appreciate the sacrifices you have made to keep us safe,' he said calmly. 'Oaths and loyalties are not things to be broken lightly. I give you my word that my crew will not mention this incident to any cartographers, mapmakers or ship-to-ship sales-mice, should we cross paths with them.'

'Here, here!' Horace chanted. 'No talking to the cart guys.' He prodded Fred with his hook. 'Got it, big fella?'

Fred looked like he'd just fallen asleep and woken up again.

'Talk to who about what?' he muttered. 'All I know is there are two maps. We've got one and the other one is …'

'Turning to dust,' the Hermit said, pulling the paper scraps from his bag. 'Windy, windy island not kind to maps. Hermit arranged copy for his son … just in case.'

The Captain glared at Rat Bait. 'I wish I knew that *before* I handed over my gold.'

Rat Bait looked sideways in guilt and Pete stamped his pencil in annoyance.

'Err, shouldn't we be focusing on deciphering the riddle?' Horace said, trying to ease the tension. 'The sooner we can find the treasure, the sooner we can get out of here and live happily ever after!'

'It's not a fairytale, you delirious dwarf,' Pete snapped. 'There are still Cat Fish on the island, remember?'

'So?' Horace retorted. 'They're probably still recovering from *jelly-tart-itis*. Besides, they have no idea where the treasure is.'

Pete screwed up his nose. 'Neither do we! All that gobbledygook you heard about the key was just a ruse to trap our timid teacher friend. The teeth on the key are no more than random shapes!'

Horace slumped his shoulders in disappointment. 'Rotten pies to random shapes!'

'So what's our next move?' Ruby asked impatiently. 'Chit-chatting in a corridor won't get us anywhere.'

'Right ye be,' Rat Bait concurred, before the Captain could answer. 'Might I suggest a bit o' friendly competition to get the mind workin'?'

'What *kind* of competition?' Horace enquired, suddenly perking up.

Rat Bait stuck his paw in his coat pocket and fumbled around for a moment.

'Aye,' he muttered to himself. 'There still be a few left.' He removed his paw and held out three gold coins. 'The first rat, weasel or mouse to discover the location o' the treasure will receive me three remainin' coins as a reward for their efforts.'

'How very generous of you,' the Captain said

sarcastically.

'I'm in!' Horace exclaimed. 'There's nothing wrong with a bit of healthy rivalry and certainly nothing wrong with the Captain's gold!'

'Very well,' Pete said. 'If we're all agreed, I'll bring the key and map into the mess room. If no one deciphers the riddle, Rat Bait's gold goes into the kitty and we sail out of here at first light.'

The crew gathered around the dining table, eager to discover the treasure's secret location. The Forgotten Map and the King's Key lay in full view for all to see. Pete's rough tracing of the map completed the mix.

While the rest of the crew concentrated on the map of the island, Whisker focused on the key. He'd spent enough time examining the Forgotten Map to know the position of every painted boulder and every pine tree. Even the words of the riddle were etched in his mind:

Uncover the key and enlighten your mind,
but wisdom is found in the shadows behind.

With the last two lines running through his head, he picked up the key and studied its painted surface closely.

Starting at the Rock of Hope, he ran his eyes up the river to the boulders and across to the letter X. He saw nothing out of the ordinary. The rest of the key appeared to be painted solely to complete the map – nothing more, nothing less.

There has to be more, he pondered, flipping the key over. The reverse side was painted black.

Wisdom is found in the shadows behind? he thought. *There's no wisdom here – only black paint and a couple of small scratches.*

He peered at the position of the scratches, hoping their placement was significant. They weren't. The scratches were no more than random wear-and-tear marks, a result of rubbing on the chameleon's neck.

Whisker turned his attention to the teeth of the key and wondered if Pete and the Captain had missed something. He rotated the key so the shaft was horizontal. The tooth closest to the handle looked like a letter *T* or a backwards letter *J*. The second tooth resembled a lightning bolt or a sideways *S*. The third tooth appeared to be a letter *Y* or a backwards number *4*.

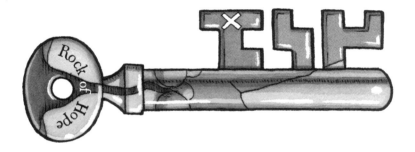

He ran through the possible combinations in his head ... *TSY ... JS4 ... T Lightning 4 ... J Lightning Y ...*

None of the sequences made any sense and the initials didn't stand for anything he knew. He felt his frustration growing. The sound of Pete sniffling next to him added to his annoyance.

'Are you going to hog that key all evening, or can the rest of us take a look at it?' Pete huffed.

Whisker handed the key straight to him.

'It's all yours, Pete,' he muttered, standing up from his chair. 'I've found it far from *enlightening*.' He was hungry and hoped supper might revitalise his mind.

As he walked to the galley he noticed that he wasn't the only one who'd taken a break. Ruby and the Hermit were playing a board game with shells on a serving bench, Eaton and Emmie were drawing with Pete's pencil stubs on the floor, Smudge was sleeping on a rafter and Fred was nowhere to be seen.

The Hermit grabbed Whisker's left sleeve on his way past and thrust something into his paw. Whisker looked down to see the Hermit's brown bag.

'W-what's this?' he asked, puzzled.

'Hermit's thank you present for saving him on the cliff,' the Hermit replied.

'I can't take this,' Whisker gasped, trying to hand the bag back to the Hermit. 'It's all you've got.'

The Hermit pushed Whisker's paw away and shook his head. 'Hermit has much more than bag of possessions, yes, yes. Hermit has his life back.' He lowered his voice and chuckled, 'Hermit's compass extremely handy for lost apprentices on cloudy nights.'

'Fair call,' Whisker muttered, hoping Ruby wasn't following the conversation. 'But don't you want to keep the bag?'

The Hermit shook his head. 'No, no! Hermit has nothing to tie it to! Whisker has fine pie-buckled belt.'

'Thanks,' Whisker said, hesitantly accepting the bag and its contents. 'I'll try to use it wisely.'

The Hermit went back to his game. Whisker fastened the bag to his belt and entered the galley. Fred stood next to the open pantry door, staring lovingly at a piece of mouldy cheese. Whisker could smell its pungent odour from across the room. It smelt worse than raw onion.

'Hi, Fred,' Whisker said. 'Have you got any pie crusts I can nibble on? I've been on island rations for days.'

Fred appeared lost in his own thoughts.

'I love cheese!' he said dreamily. 'But it always gives me a belly ache.'

'Oh,' Whisker said. 'Maybe that's because you're lactose intolerant.'

Fred looked hurt.

'You think I'm *lacking in tolerance*?' he asked, confused.

'No, no, of course not,' Whisker said, trying to recover. 'Lactose intolerant means you're allergic to *dairy*. All rats are.'

'Really?' Fred said, downcast. 'Well in that case, cheese is no longer my friend.' He wrapped the sticky object in a piece of cloth and handed it to Whisker. 'Take it out of my sight!'

'S-sure,' Whisker said awkwardly. 'I'll feed it to the scorpions … or maybe the owls? They'll eat anything – and anyone!' He slipped the cheese into his new bag.

Handy already, he thought to himself.

'Now, Fred,' he said, 'how about those snacks?'

Fred opened the enormous wood-fired oven and pulled out a large tray of piping-hot pesto party pies.

'Cooked to perfection!' he said proudly. 'I hope you're hungry?'

Whisker decided there were more than enough pies to share with the rest of the crew and carried three heaped serving platters into the mess room. It was a clumsy task with only two small paws, but his tail helped out as best it could.

He tried to navigate past Pete, who was scribbling frantically with his pencil, while spinning the key in circles with his paws.

'SUPPER IS SERVED!' Fred shouted from the galley.

Pete jumped in surprise and snapped the lead of his red pencil. Trying to stay upright, he stumbled backwards and collided with Whisker. Three dishes of pies soared into the air.

CLANG! SPLAT! SPLAT! CLANG! RATTLE! SPLAT!

Half-a-dozen pies landed on Pete's drawing. The remainder of the pies hit the white walls of the mess room, breaking open on impact. Oily green filling sprayed everywhere.

'Oh dear!' Fred gasped, from the galley door. 'Oh double dear!'

Pete was furious.

'What the flaming rat's tail are you doing?' he shouted, scraping pesto from his bony white nose.

Whisker picked up Pete's broken lead and handed it to the irate Quartermaster. 'Ooops … sorry.'

'Sorry doesn't cut it!' Pete fumed, wedging the lead into Whisker's bag. 'You can keep the stupid lead! Do you know how hard it is to get a pencil the right length?'

'No.'

'It's *extremely* hard! I can't just sharpen it – one leg will be shorter than the other! My favourite red pencil is ruined!' He looked down at his drawing. 'And so is my masterful work!'

Pete angrily waved his bony paws in the air. 'I nearly had it, you know. A few more characters and I would have cracked the code. But look at it now: One big soggy slop! There's no way I'll uncover a single word with pesto painted all over it …'

Whisker didn't hear the rest of Pete's tirade – there was no need. Pete had just solved the riddle without even knowing it.

SIXTEEN

In the Shadows Behind

Whisker grabbed the key from Pete, mid-rant.

'Hey!' Pete snapped. 'You've had your turn.'

'So have you,' Whisker said, throwing the key to Ruby.

Ruby caught it and frowned. 'What am I supposed to do with this? I hate riddles. Riddles are words, words, words and no action.' She threw the key back to Whisker like it was a hot pie.

'Action is exactly what we're missing,' Whisker said, catching the key with his tail.

He picked up Eaton's lantern from the floor, shutting its three mirrored sides and held the key in front of the remaining open side.

'We're supposed to *uncover the key*,' Whisker explained. 'But technically it was never covered up – or so we thought. Take a look at the key and tell me what you see.'

Horace stuck his face in front of the lantern.

'I see the dark silhouette of a key surrounded by an extremely bright light that's hurting my eyes,' he said.

'What else?' Whisker asked.

'A couple of tiny rust spots,' Horace said. 'They must be pretty deep. The light is shining straight through.'

152

'So what?' Pete snapped. 'The key was in a rainforest for years. A bit of rust is inevitable.'

'And I would agree with you,' Whisker said haughtily, 'except these are not rust holes.'

'Well, what are they?' Pete exclaimed. 'Worm holes?'

Horace ran his nail over the surface of the key. 'They feel solid.'

'Exactly!' Whisker said.

Mr Tribble tilted his spectacles and peered closer.

'Glass?' he considered.

'It could be,' Whisker replied. 'We discovered three substances among the blacksmith's equipment in the citadel dungeon. One was gold from the false key, one was brass from the King's Key and the other was a clear substance that resembled glass.'

The Captain looked astonished. 'So you're saying there's a transparent layer of glass beneath the painted surface?'

'It would fit with the riddle,' Mr Tribble replied. 'The word *enlighten* contains the word *light*. A hidden layer would be found *behind* the painted surface – in the *shadows* so to speak.'

'There's only one way to find out,' Whisker said with a grin. 'Ruby, if you please.'

Ruby drew a scarlet scissor sword from her belt. 'Permission to commence *operation face-lift*, Captain?'

'Scrape at will, my dear,' the Captain replied.

Ruby began scratching at the surface of the key with her sword. Almost immediately, a line of symbols appeared along its central shaft. Ruby shifted her blade to the teeth of the key. As the paint flaked away, the X marks-the-spot disappeared and was replaced by three circles and a small arrowhead known as a chevron.

Ruby proceeded to scratch the black paint off the rear side of the key before giving the whole thing a quick dust off with her paw. Triumphantly, she held the newly *uncovered* King's Key in front of the lantern.

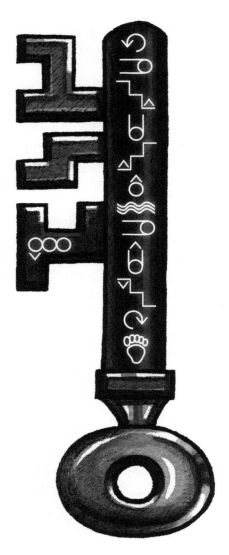

The light streamed through a dozen miniature glass symbols. Some looked like tunnels, others like stairs. There were circles and arrows, lines and squiggles. The final symbol was a right-handed paw.

'Argh me pastries!' Horace exclaimed, pointing to the paw with his hook. 'I'm sure I saw a symbol like that in the citadel. It was on the doorway to the throne room ... or was it the dungeon?'

'Both,' Mr Tribble replied knowledgeably. 'The right paw of royalty was on the doorway to the throne room. The left paw of despair – also the symbol for the great brown bear – was at the entrance to the dungeon.

'The paws weren't the only symbols we saw in the citadel,' the Captain added. 'We saw scores of symbols matching the ones on the key at the tops of doorways.'

'Freeforian cave symbols, to be precise,' Mr Tribble said. 'They're part of an ancient underground navigation system.'

'Do we know what all the symbols stand for?' Pete asked.

'I can identify a couple of them,' Madam Pearl said, moving closer. 'I've seen them on Freeforian antiques, particularly oil lamps. The rest are a mystery to me.'

'But not to *me*,' Mr Tribble said proudly. 'I took the liberty of recording every symbol from the citadel in my notebook. Each symbol is matched with its meaning. The notebook is in my sleeping quarters, if you'd like me to find it?'

'We'd *love* you to find it!' Horace exclaimed. 'Why play the guessing game when there's a know-it-all in the crew?'

Mr Tribble straightened his glasses and hurried from the room. The rest of the crew crowded around the key.

155

The Captain pointed to the small symbol on the tooth of the key.

'If I'm interpreting this correctly,' he said, 'the X never marked the location of the treasure; it marked the entrance to a maze of tunnels and passages inside the mountain. The symbols on the shaft tell us which passages to take. The last symbol, the right paw, must mark the treasure's location.'

The Hermit looked perplexed. 'Hermit never knew about secret tunnels on Mt Mobziw, no, no. Many caves on Mt Moochup where Hermit lived, yes, yes, but only owls on Mt Mobziw!'

'It appears someone has gone to great lengths to keep the entrance a secret,' the Captain said, his eye still fixed on the key.

There was a scuffle of small feet and Whisker looked up to see Mr Tribble returning to the room carrying his notebook and several sheets of paper.

'I thought Emmie and Eaton might like to help me interpret these symbols,' Mr Tribble said. 'It's far more enthralling than last term's school project on humpback whale calls!'

Emmie clapped her paws together in excitement. Eaton looked his usual nervous self but with an extra dose of jitters.

Mr Tribble handed the children a sheet of paper and several pencil stubs. He opened his notebook and flicked to the page of symbols. Madam Pearl held the key in front of the lantern and Emmie copied down the first symbol, while Eaton squirmed uncomfortably in his chair.

'C-can I have my own sheet of paper, please?' he asked timidly. 'Emmie always hogs the pencils.'

'Do not!' Emmie squeaked, hogging the pencils.

Mr Tribble sighed and handed Eaton a blank sheet of paper.

Pete gave Eaton a purple pencil stub and whispered, 'It's always good to have a backup, young mouse. Sooner or later, some clumsy buffoon will go and lose the original.' He looked directly at Whisker and smirked.

Whisker smiled back politely. There was no point arguing. He'd lost the key *and* the map on more than one occasion. Fortunately for Whisker, he was rather adept at getting them back.

The children raced to be the first mouse finished, carefully matching each symbol from the key with its interpretation from the notebook.

'Me money's on the wee lad 'ere,' Rat Bait chuckled. 'He's got a fierce look 'o determination in his eye!'

'But Emmie's quicker with her paw-writing,' Horace argued.

In the end it was a dead heat. Thanks to Mr Tribble's thorough recording skills, the mice managed to find an interpretation for every symbol.

'Our first task is to locate a line of three rocks,' the Captain said, summing up their discoveries. 'The chevron would indicate there's something under the rock on the left.'

'A lever, perhaps?' Mr Tribble suggested, pointing to the first symbol on the shaft of the key. 'Something that requires an anti-clockwise turn.'

'The rest of the directions appear straightforward enough,' the Captain continued. 'Left, up, through, right, over, etcetera, etcetera ... a clockwise turn and we're there!'

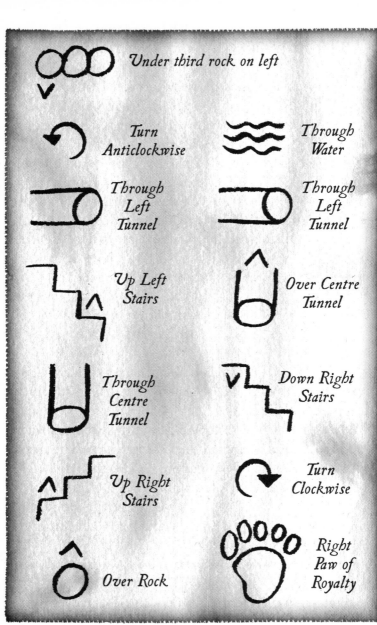

Under third rock on left

Turn Anticlockwise

Through Water

Through Left Tunnel

Through Left Tunnel

Up Left Stairs

Over Centre Tunnel

Through Centre Tunnel

Down Right Stairs

Up Right Stairs

Turn Clockwise

Over Rock

Right Paw of Royalty

'So when do we leave?' Ruby asked, tapping her nails on the table.

Pete screwed up his nose. 'Not until that cursed Cat Fish crew have sailed off into the sunset! They'll be waiting to ambush us for sure.'

The Hermit shook his head. 'Quartermaster Pete has nothing to worry about, no, no. Cat Fish will be too busy bailing water from *Sinking Sardine*.'

'*Sinking Sardine?*' Horace echoed.

'Yes, yes!' the Hermit chuckled. 'Hermit visited *Sinking Sardine* earlier this evening. Diving gear exceptional. Kitchen can-opener outstanding! Tomorrow, Cat Fish will wake to find *Sinking Sardine* submerged in lagoon.'

'A splendid piece of news!' the Captain laughed heartily. 'We'll leave at first light.' He grew serious and eyed his crew. 'An expedition of this nature requires plenty of weapons and plenty of supplies. I expect all crew members to be fully prepared. There's not a moment to lose.'

'Aye, aye, Captain!' chanted the crew.

The Captain strode from the room, stopping momentarily under the doorway. Smudge was busily sucking pesto from the wall.

'And for Ratbeard's sake,' the Captain groaned, 'will someone clean up this ghastly green goop before it attracts an entire island of insects?'

Whisker knew *someone* meant the rat responsible for the mess. He begrudgingly raised his paw to volunteer.

Emmie tugged on his shirt.

'You'll need a qualified hygiene officer to supervise,' she squeaked.

'Thanks, Emmie,' Whisker said gratefully. 'You assess the damage and I'll get the scrubbing brushes.'

While Whisker fetched a large pot of water and two scrubbing brushes from the galley, the crew dispersed to prepare for the adventure.

Whisker returned to find Emmie wiping pesto from Pete's pencils and Eaton staring at the key.

'Come to lend a paw, Eaton?' Whisker asked.

Eaton gave Whisker a horrified look and dashed from the room, clutching a pile of crumpled paper in one paw and his lantern in the other.

'That's Eaton's attempt at cleaning up!' Emmie squeaked. 'He'll never make a good hygiene officer.'

Lighthouses

It took several hours for Whisker and Emmie to clean the oily green stains from the walls. From time to time another member of the crew would pass through the mess room on their way to the pantry. Whisker wondered how much food the expedition actually required.

'You can never have too many snacks if you're stuck in a mountain,' Horace said on his third trip past. 'Besides, not all of this is for eating.'

He held up two rubber sauce bottles.

'Hot chilli sauce shooters,' he boasted. 'I picked them from the retirement resort gift shop. They came filled with tomato sauce, but I added the hot chillies for an extra kick! They're equipped with non-clog nozzles and rapid-fire squeezable sides.' He lowered the bright red bottles to his hips like a gunslinger. 'I can give you a demonstration if you like? See that white wall over there ...'

'Err, that's ok, Horace,' Whisker said uneasily. 'I'd prefer it if *one* wall stayed white.'

Horace let out a long sigh of disappointment and was nearly knocked over by Ruby, bursting into the mess room. Horace, in turn, pretended to squirt her with his sauce shooters. She ignored his antics and opened her paw to reveal a crumpled scarlet eye patch.

Horace's jaw dropped wide open.

'Rotten pies!' he gasped. 'How could we be so blind?'

Whisker's tail collapsed into the pot of green cleaning water.

'But that means …'

'Aye,' Ruby said coldly. 'In all the excitement, we overlooked one crucial fact: Mr Tribble may be innocent, but there's still a thief onboard and they know exactly where the treasure is!'

'Rotten pies with mouldy pastry!' Horace cried.

He glanced down at the table. The Forgotten Map lay next to the King's Key and Emmie's drawing of the symbols.

'Phew!' he sighed, calming down. 'At least they don't have the map and the key.'

Whisker didn't share his relief.

'Take another look,' he said, grimly. 'Eaton's page of symbols and Pete's tracing are gone.'

'Rotten pies with mouldy pastry *and* curdled cream!' Horace gasped.

'Speaking of Eaton,' Ruby said in a panic, 'where is the little mouse?'

Emmie looked up from her scrubbing brush.

'I haven't seen him for hours,' she replied with a shrug. 'But he could be on the deck with his lantern. He's often up there at night playing his little game of lanterns and lighthouses. I'm not sure of the rules – he never lets me join in!'

The blood drained from Whisker's soggy tail. Ruby stared at him in horror and let out an angry *HISS*.

'What?' Horace cried, clearly missing something.

Before Whisker could relay his grave fears, Mr Tribble strode into the room, clutching an empty bottle of lantern oil.

'Has anyone seen …?' He cut himself short when he saw the sea of worried faces.

'Oh my,' he gasped. 'Is something wrong?'

'Yes,' Ruby said bluntly. 'We have a situation.'

'W-what kind of situation?' Mr Tribble murmured.

'A spy situation,' Ruby replied.

'But who?' he whispered, turning pale.

Ruby looked at Whisker for a tactful answer.

Whisker took a deep breath. *No more false accusations,* he told himself. *You have to be certain.*

'Mr Tribble,' he said with an air of urgency, 'tell us everything you know about Eaton's lantern.'

'Eaton's lantern?' Mr Tribble gasped. 'You're not suggesting … surely not? Eaton's just a boy.'

Emmie rushed forward and buried her head in his chest, tears filling her small eyes. Mr Tribble put a comforting arm around her.

'I'm not suggesting anything,' Whisker said calmly. 'I'm just looking for facts.'

Mr Tribble stared at him for a long time and then hesitantly nodded. 'Alright, I'll tell you what I know. As I'm sure you're already aware, Whisker, the lantern was purchased from Salamander's Splendid Supplies on Sea Shanty Island on the night you escaped from the Cat Fish. Earlier that evening, the Captain gave Fred enough money to buy the children each a small gift – following our unfortunate boat disaster. At the time of entering the supply store, Emmie wanted a box of candy canes and Eaton had his heart set on a survival knot handbook. By the time the rest of the Pie Rats arrived looking for Sabre, Eaton had changed his mind to a lantern. He's always been afraid of the dark, so I thought nothing of it.'

'We found Eaton in the lantern aisle when we entered the shop,' Horace added. 'He was by himself and acting extremely jittery.'

'There's no denying that Sabre and Master Meow entered and exited the shop while Fred and the mice were in there,' Whisker said. 'I saw that from my hiding spot in the drain. The question is: what happened in between?'

'I saw and heard nothing,' Mr Tribble said firmly. 'None of us did. Emmie was upstairs with Fred and I presume Eaton was in the lantern aisle the entire time.'

'What part of the store is the lantern aisle?' Whisker asked.

'Ground floor, near the back door,' Ruby said. 'The same door Sabre exited through.'

Mr Tribble put his head in his paws. The evidence was mounting.

Whisker continued his questioning. 'Does Eaton know any *signal codes* – messages using short and long flashes of light?'

Mr Tribble lifted his head and nodded. 'He's the best in his class.'

'I'm guessing a mirrored lantern would be the obvious choice for long range signalling,' Whisker said. 'The narrow beam would make it visible from miles away – like a lighthouse.'

'Quite so,' Mr Tribble said, downcast. 'Eaton's lantern would be perfect.'

'Putrid pastries,' Horace muttered. 'I feel sick in the gizzards. Eaton had oodles of opportunities to signal the

Cat Fish. First Sea Shanty Island, then Prison Island ... Shipwreck Sandbar ... even the jungle citadel ... It's no wonder they knew our every move.'

'H-hold on a minute,' Mr Tribble quivered. 'We don't know for certain it was Eaton. He could simply be watching the stars innocently from –'

'– the deck?' Pete broke in.

Whisker turned to see the agitated quartermaster clomping into the room, followed by the rest of the crew. Pete held several strands of maroon thread between his fingers.

'Recognise these, anyone?'

Emmie buried her nose further into Mr Tribble's chest.

'Where did you get those?' Mr Tribble gasped.

'At the end of the rope,' Pete said coldly. 'The Hermit was hauling supplies onto the cliff top when he discovered a couple of stray fibres. We were naturally worried the Cat Fish had snuck aboard and took the liberty of searching the entire ship. Unless Eaton's hiding in the pantry, he's already on the island.'

Pete held the maroon strands against Emmie's school blazer.

'A perfect colour match,' he remarked. 'It seems our traitor was a snivelling mouse after all!'

'How dare you!' Mr Tribble squeaked in anger.

Pete narrowed his pink albino eyes. 'Eaton had the means ...'

'But his motive remains a mystery,' the Captain cut in. 'Now is not the time for passing judgement, Pete. Is that understood?'

'Aye, Captain,' Pete said reluctantly.

'Our focus is to stop Eaton before he reaches the Cat

Fish,' the Captain went on. 'Failing that, our priority will be to rescue him and bring him back alive. Regardless of Eaton's intentions, he is still an honorary member of our crew and under my direct protection.'

He scanned the eyes of his crew. 'We'll split into three groups and search the island. Each group will be led by a rat familiar with the landscape. I'll lead the first group of Pete, Fred, Horace and Smudge to the camp on the beach. It's the most likely place Eaton will be headed, but also the most dangerous.'

He ran his finger over the Forgotten Map from east to west.

'Whisker will lead Ruby and the mice to the treasure site on Mt Mobziw.' He looked directly at Ruby. 'If you spot the Cat Fish, you are to wait for backup. Is that understood?'

Ruby gave a reluctant sigh. 'And if the place is deserted?'

'You have permission to enter the mountain,' the Captain replied. 'If the treasure is as powerful as the legend claims, it may help us to defeat the Cat Fish, or at least secure Eaton's release.'

The Captain pointed further up the island.

'The Hermit and Madam Pearl will head into owl territory and work their way down the mountain. The Hermit knows the terrain better than anyone and owls are less likely to attack with a weasel present.'

Mr Tribble shuddered. 'You don't think the owls have taken Eaton, do you?'

'Nothing's certain,' the Captain replied. 'But time is against us. Travel light. Bring only the weapons you need. We leave immediately.' He turned to go.

'Excuse me, Capt'n,' Rat Bait croaked. 'Ye be forgettin' 'bout me.'

'I haven't forgotten anything,' the Captain hissed over his shoulder. 'You're not part of the plan, Rat Bait. I need rats I can rely on!'

'B-but,' Rat Bait protested. 'I can hold me own in a fight an' ...'

The Captain disappeared out the door before Rat Bait could finish.

The old rogue gave Whisker a pleading look. 'Surely *ye* trust me, Whisker?'

Whisker knew Rat Bait was a valuable asset in any confrontation. The disgraced Pie Rat had nothing to lose but everything to prove. He was sly, strong, and, most importantly, he wasn't a spy.

'What do you think, Ruby?' Whisker muttered.

'We need a bodyguard for the mice,' Ruby whispered back. 'Give the scoundrel the job if you think he's up to it.'

Whisker gestured to Rat Bait. 'You're on mouse duty, Rat Bait. Keep your eye out for scorpions, your nose open for Cat Fish ...'

'And your mouth shut,' Ruby snapped.

'Aye,' Rat Bait said, putting his strong paws on Emmie's shoulders. 'I won't let ye down.'

'You'd better not,' Ruby hissed. 'You've already had your second chance. I doubt the Captain will give you a third.'

EIGHTEEN

East to West

One by one, the Pie Rats scrambled up the crude rope to the top of the cliff. Pale stars flickered overhead in the moonless sky. A brisk wind blew from the East, slicing through the tense air. The crew gathered in a silent huddle for their final instructions.

'Crew first, treasure second,' the Captain said with resolve. 'If you run into trouble, hoot like an owl. If you run into an owl, hiss like a cat!'

With whispers of 'Aye, aye, Captain,' the parties separated.

Horace gave Whisker a farewell salute with his hook and scurried after the Captain with sauce bottles bulging from his belt.

Whisker hoped he'd see his friend again. It had been a whirlwind few hours since his rescue on the ledge, and the last thing he wanted was to lose the crew all over again.

As the danger of the mission sank in, Whisker was glad he had Ruby by his side. He knew she'd prefer to be fighting with her fellow crew-rats than trailing after an apprentice, but her lack of protest was a comfort. Whatever they faced, they faced together.

Whisker's team set off to the north-west, travelling with

Madam Pearl and the Hermit. The plan was to journey as far as the Hermit's cave, at which point they would split up and go in different directions. Whisker had the stars and the Hermit's compass to guide him – neither of which he needed while the Hermit was present.

Ruby and Rat Bait carried small ship's lanterns. They were considerably dimmer than Eaton's mirrored lantern, but ideal for creeping unseen across the island.

Emmie was understandably distraught following Eaton's suspected betrayal and hadn't stopped sobbing since they left. Although Emmie and Eaton were like cheese and chalk, Eaton was still Emmie's twin, and the news of his treachery had hit her hard. Whisker wondered how she would cope if they got to him too late.

The sombre party reached the outskirts of boulder country and made their way into the rocky foothills. Grey stones surrounded them like expressionless faces, bleak and unwelcoming. Emmie's tiny legs quickly grew tired from leaping over crevices and scaling boulders and Rat Bait resorted to carrying her on his back.

The companions neared the Hermit's cave with no sightings of scorpions, owls, Cat Fish or wandering mice. From the tops of high boulders, they looked down at the lagoon. Not a single light radiated from the beach camp and there were no signs of activity on the *Silver Sardine*. From a dark distance, it was impossible to tell how far the ship's hull was submerged under the jet black water.

'Them crafty cats could be anywhere,' Rat Bait croaked.

'We've got to keep moving,' Ruby said forcefully. 'There's no time to waste on idle speculation.'

The Hermit agreed. 'Must hurry, yes, yes. Dawn

approaches. Hermit and Pearl depart for owl country now.'

'We'll see you shortly,' Madam Pearl said in a rich, confident tone. 'Have faith, Emmie. This is the Island of Destiny ...'

Emmie stopped sobbing and watched the white weasel and the wily Hermit disappear into the darkness. Whisker hoped the two companions would find nothing but an empty nest.

Whisker led Ruby, Rat Bait and the mice westwards along the ridge of boulders. He knew their path was the most exposed, but resisted the temptation to move into sheltered territory – scorpions would undoubtedly be patrolling the higher terrain.

The gurgling sounds of the mountain stream soon filled their ears, telling Whisker they had reached the very centre of the island.

The sky lightened as dawn approached. The Pie Rats extinguished their lanterns and pressed on. Spindly pine trees and stunted bushes appeared further up the mountain. Whisker directed his companions towards the wind-ravaged plants. He felt the crunch of broken rocks under his feet and knew it was only a short hike to the treasure site.

Confident of his navigation skills, he returned the compass to his bag and checked it was tied securely to his belt. He took the liberty of glancing down at the map canister and then reached his paw into his right pocket. His fingers touched the cold shaft of the King's Key.

Still there, he thought. He knew Emmie's sheet of symbols would lead them to the location of the treasure, but he couldn't stop wondering what would happen then.

Will the key open a secret door? Will it unlock a golden chest?

Whisker withdrew his paw from his pocket and began clawing his way through the bushes.

THUD! THUD! SCRAPE.

The sounds came from somewhere close. Whisker halted and raised his finger to his lips. The rodents behind him froze.

THUD! THUD! CLANG!

'More infuriating rocks!' complained a gruff voice.

Whisker peered through the gaps in the leaves to see Master Meow and Furious Fur crouched waist deep in a hole, clutching small shovels in their paws. Two boulders towered over the hole. A third boulder stood a short way off. Whisker shifted his eyes to his left and caught sight of Eaton, bound and gagged on a stump between Sally and Cleopatra.

Master Meow hurled a shovelful of rocks over his shoulder.

'Ow!' Siamese Sally hissed. 'Watch where you're throwing that stuff, shovel-head! We've got a fragile prisoner over here.'

'He's not as fragile as you, princess!' Meow sniggered.

Cleopatra let out an evil laugh. 'But he's far more valuable!'

Sally slashed her claws at Cleopatra. Cleopatra leapt back as Sally's arm spun through the air, narrowly missing Eaton's head.

Eaton sat petrified on the stump, unable to move or speak, as the two cats hissed and spat at each other.

'ENOUGH!' Sabre roared furiously, stepping into Whisker's view. 'If either one of you good-for-nothing creatures lays a finger on our precious hostage, I'll turn your hide into a handbag and make a necklace from your bones. Is that understood?'

Sally and Cleopatra drew back, still glaring at each other. Master Meow resumed digging. Furious Fur stroked his shaggy, white fur and muttered, 'I'd make a lovely soft handbag.'

Sabre ignored him and turned to Eaton. 'It's a dreadful shame you couldn't fulfil your end of the bargain, little spy.' He held up two sheets of paper. 'A tracing of the map and a page of symbols are all well and good, but without the key they're merely previews of the main event. You'd better hope your pesky friends come looking for you and are stupid enough to bring the key with them. I suspect we'll see them shortly, now the sun has risen.'

Whisker felt a sudden twinge of panic race through his tail. *We're walking into a trap.*

He pulled away from the bushes, hoping the Cat Fish hadn't caught his scent, and silently gestured for his friends to retreat.

Rat Bait and the mice moved instantly but Ruby gave him a look that said, *we can take them,* and held her ground.

Whisker shook his head and mouthed, *Captain's orders,* and followed the others through the bushes. Ruby finally backed down and trailed after him.

Quieter than a school of frozen fish in an iceberg, the escaping group made their way up the mountainside where the cover was dense, only stopping when they reached a thicket of pine trees. Several large boulders sheltered the trees from the wind.

'What do we do now?' Mr Tribble whispered to

Whisker.

Whisker suddenly wished he wasn't the leader. He knew which mountain paths to take and he knew how to stay out of sight, but he had little experience in formulating battle plans.

'I-I don't know,' he said with a shrug. 'Eaton's safe as long as we have the key and the treasure remains hidden.'

'It won't stay hidden for long,' Ruby said candidly. 'I doubt they have much further to dig.'

Emmie gasped.

'Maybe they be diggin' in the wrong location?' Rat Bait said. 'One o' the boulders wasn't touchin' the others.'

'I doubt we'll find three boulders closer than that,' Ruby shot back. 'I tell you, we need to get –' She stopped.

There was a rustling noise from the closest tree. The three rats drew their swords.

Prowler, Whisker thought, his tail beginning to shiver. *He wasn't with the others.*

The rats crept closer to investigate, forming a tight semicircle around the trunk. Mr Tribble covered Emmie's eyes as the rats raised their swords, preparing to strike.

The rustling suddenly stopped. Whisker prodded the branches with his blade. Nothing stirred.

'It just be the wind,' Rat Bait whispered.

'Or a large, green blowfly,' Ruby said, relieved.

She pointed into the air with her sword. Hovering a few feet from the tree and quietly beating his wings was Smudge.

The rats breathed a collective sigh of relief and lowered their weapons. Smudge landed on a rock next to them.

'The Cat Fish are at the treasure site with Eaton,' Whisker relayed. 'Is the Captain on his way?'

Smudge nodded.

'Tell him to approach from the western flank,' Ruby said, taking charge of the situation. 'We'll attack from the east.'

Smudge looked around to get his bearings.

'Don't worry, I'll show you the precise location,' Whisker said. He scrambled up the side of a boulder for a better vantage point and Ruby and Smudge joined him at the top.

Whisker handed the map to Ruby and took out the compass. He turned it in his paw until the needle pointed north and peered over the edge of the boulder.

'The Cat Fish are south-west of here,' he whispered, 'just beyond those bushes. I suggest the Captain comes up through the lower pine forest on the western side of the mountain and then heads inland.'

He raised his head and scanned the distant western shoreline, spotting a blurry rock island off the coast. He checked its direction on the compass.

'Your eyes are better than mine, Smudge, so you won't have any trouble using that island as your marker. It has similar latitude to the treasure site. You'll need to progress through the forest until you draw level with the island. If you reach the owl cliffs, you've gone too far. From there it's a simple east-north-east march to the treasure site to ensure you have the high ground advantage.'

Whisker thought he'd explained his directions clearly, but Smudge raised four arms as if to say *huh?*

'Show him on the map,' Ruby said impatiently.

'Alright,' Whisker sighed. He pointed to the map in Ruby's paws. 'Here's the beach. Here's the forest. The treasure site is located at the bottom tooth of the key and the small island is …' He paused and looked at the map, perplexed. '… the island is on the opposite side of the map.'

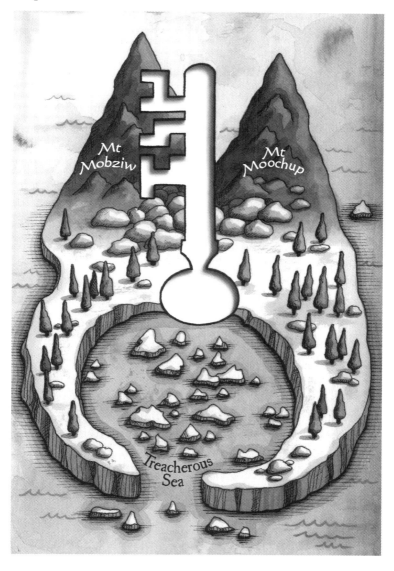

'It can't be,' Ruby said. 'We sailed straight through those waters. There's definitely nothing there. There's only one island and it's to the *west* of the mainland, not the *east*.'

'You don't need to convince me!' Whisker said, shaking his head. I can see the real island with my own eyes. It must be a mistake.'

The tip of Mr Tribble's nose appeared halfway up the side of the boulder.

'Mistake?' he said. 'I assure you I copied the map correctly in every detail.'

'Except the three sets of waves,' Ruby muttered.

'That was a stylistic alteration,' Mr Tribble said defensively. 'The island is identical.'

'Identical to the original map, maybe,' Whisker said, running his finger over the coastline, 'but not the actual island. I hadn't noticed it before, but the secret cove is drawn on the opposite coast and I swear the eastern mountain should be higher than the western one.'

'East, west, north, south! There's not even a stupid directional symbol,' Ruby said in a condescending voice.

'You're right,' Whisker said. 'We just presumed the top of the map was north.'

'You didn't presume anything,' Mr Tribble said in frustration, reaching the top of the boulder. 'The compass in your paw tells you which way is north!'

'But it also tells me which way is east and west,' Whisker said.

'So north is north and south is south but east is west and west is east,' Ruby snapped. 'Who cares? We're wasting time on insignificant details when we could be planning an ambush.'

'None of this is insignificant,' Whisker said. 'Don't you

both see that?'

Smudge raised his arms as if to say *I do!*

Whisker continued, 'The Island of Destiny is almost symmetrical. If we hadn't discovered these small details we would never know –'

'That the map is drawn in reverse!' Mr Tribble exclaimed, his eyes lighting up with a sudden realisation. 'Turn it over and see.'

Ruby flipped the map over and held it up to the morning sun. Light streamed through the yellowed paper, revealing the entire map as a mirror image. The small island lay to the west, the sheltered cove hugged the eastern coastline and the tallest mountain rose to the east. Exactly as it should appear.

Whisker removed the King's Key from his pocket and inserted in into the key-shaped hole in the map. In reverse, the symbols took on new meaning – right became left, clockwise became anticlockwise.

While the words of the map appeared as indecipherable scrawl, one word took on a new meaning. Standing out against the dark shadow of the eastern mountain was a white-lettered word. It had once read *Mobziw*. Now it read *wisdoM*

'... *wisdom is found in the shadows behind,*' Whisker recited.

'We have been *enlightened!*' Mr Tribble marvelled. 'We looked and looked but it is only now that we truly *see*. No wonder the treasure has remained hidden. We had the wrong mountain all along.'

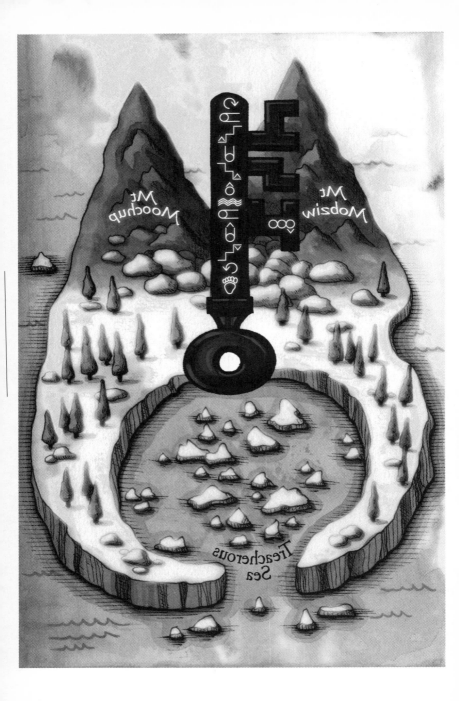

NINETEEN

The Other Mountain

The startling discovery called for immediate action. According to the reversed map, the secret entrance to the mountain of wisdom was located directly north of the Hermit's lair. Whisker knew they could reach it in less time than it took the Captain to trek through the forest. He also knew that embarking on a treasure hunt meant leaving Eaton at the mercy of the Cat Fish. It was a choice he didn't want to make.

In the end, Mr Tribble made it for him.

'I am responsible for all of your safety,' he said, putting a paw on Emmie's shoulder, 'and for Eaton's. If we attack the Cat Fish in broad daylight, there will be casualties – Eaton may be one of them. If we hand over the key, we have no guarantee they will spare any of us. But if we find the treasure, we might just have a chance of ending this peacefully ...' He choked up.

'There, there,' Rat Bait said, trying to comfort him. 'Sabre cares more 'bout the treasure than eatin' the wee lad. No 'arm will come to Eaton while we're in the mountain. Mark me words.'

Whisker couldn't bring himself to say anything. Rat Bait's logic made perfect sense, as did Mr Tribble's, but

179

Whisker felt he had a duty that went beyond logic – a duty to rescue Eaton even if he perished in the process. That was the price of loyalty. Ruby looked uncomfortable, too. She was never one to shy away from a fight.

Mr Tribble looked from Whisker to Ruby as if reading their thoughts.

'Not today, young rats,' he said, sounding like an overprotective school teacher. 'Be patient. The time for battles will come.'

It took Ruby a moment to agree with him, but when she did, there was no going back.

'We head for the treasure,' she said decisively. 'Smudge, tell the Captain to meet us on the eastern mountain. Give the same message to the Hermit if you cross paths with him. Whisker, lead the way.'

Without further discussion, Smudge disappeared into the cloudless sky and Whisker led the others down the slope of the western mountain. The treasure hunters backtracked along the weathered boulders, heading east past the mountain spring. It was an easier journey in daylight, even with a stiff headwind. Whisker hoped any lingering onion odours weren't reaching the Cat Fish.

They arrived in the general vicinity of the Hermit's lair and, after a couple of minutes of searching, located its concealed entrance. The companions piled inside and threw themselves onto the ground to catch their breaths.

The confinement of the cave felt strangely comforting to Whisker. The dangers of the island were momentarily blocked by solid walls of rock arching above his head.

Emmie discovered several piles of pine nuts in the corner of the cave and divided them among the hungry rodents. She made no attempt to offer anyone the mouldy onions from the opposite corner. With renewed strength, they departed the cave for the next stage of their quest.

'If anything happens, we'll meet back here,' Whisker said, removing the broken pencil lead from his bag. He scratched a subtle mark on a nearby rock. 'This should help us find the entrance.'

The companions travelled due north, scaling one boulder after another. It was unfamiliar territory for Whisker. The boulders were larger and smoother than those lower down the slope, and the mountain shrubs were shrivelled and lifeless. Whisker had his suspicions that scorpions would be hidden in many of the dark crevices they passed.

Withered thistles began to appear in the rocky, black soil between boulders. Whisker guessed they were close to the *true* treasure site.

'Look out for a group of three boulders,' he said. 'It might take some hunting, but don't give up. They'll be here somewhere.'

Ruby pointed directly behind Whisker. 'Do you mean three boulders like those?'

Whisker turned to see three round boulders in a tight row.

'Err, that could be them ...' Whisker said, embarrassed.

Mr Tribble took out Emmie's symbol sheet.

'We need to dig under the end boulder,' he said.

'Remember the symbols are reversed,' Ruby pointed out.

'Yes, I'm aware of that,' Mr Tribble said emphatically. 'It would seem the boulder on the right is our target. It appears slightly squarer than the other two boulders – like a doorway.'

'There's only one way to find out,' Ruby said, pulling

out one of her swords.

With powerful blows of her blade, she began hacking at the hard ground. Whisker and Rat Bait joined in with their own scissor swords. Ruby handed Mr Tribble her second sword and Emmie found a strong shard of rock to use. Together they broke up the soil and scooped out the loose fragments with their paws.

No one doubted a good shovel or two would make the job a much swifter process, and the rodents' arms quickly grew tired. To save their strength, they reverted to shifts of scraping and scooping rather than all digging at once. They had dug through several centimetres of hard earth when Rat Bait's blade struck something solid.

'Over 'ere!' he exclaimed. 'I think I've found somethin'.'

Whisker and Ruby rushed over to assist. The three rats brushed away a thin layer of dirt to reveal the upper edge of a round metal object resembling a large cog or a ship's wheel. A long metal shaft ran from the centre of the wheel into the ground. The shaft was attached to the rim of the wheel by thick metal spokes.

The five companions clapped their dusty paws in triumph. There was still more scraping to do before the wheel was free from the earth, but the excited diggers made short work of the task. When the last pawful of dirt was removed from the hole, they dropped their digging implements and each took a spot along the rim of the wheel.

'The wheel requires a clockwise turn,' Mr Tribble said, reversing the symbols on Emmie's sheet. 'Let's hope the shaft hasn't rusted solid.'

'We turn on three,' Ruby instructed. 'One, two, three!'

The companions heaved, their muscles strained, but the

wheel didn't budge. They tried again, with greater effort – still no success.

'We need more leverage,' Whisker puffed. 'If we insert our sword blades through the holes in the wheel, we can use them to pry the wheel forward.'

'It's worth a try,' Ruby agreed.

The four swords were spaced around the wheel. Each blade passed through a hole on an angle, its tip digging into the ground.

'On my cue, pull your sword towards you like a lever,' Whisker instructed. 'The straightening blade should turn the wheel. Ready? Now!'

The rodents pulled with all their strength. There was a sharp *CREAK* from the shaft as the wheel began to turn. At the same time, the sound of grating stone filled their ears and the boulder on the right slowly swivelled into the mountain.

The blades of the swords straightened. The excited treasure hunters paused, panting for breath, and looked across at the boulder. It had rotated several centimetres. A small gap had appeared to its left. Cold, musty air seeped out.

'Keep pulling,' Ruby said. 'Not even Smudge would fit through that gap!'

The swords were repositioned and the heaving began again. The boulder turned further, widening the gap. The companions repeated the process again and again, their muscles burning with every attempt. The boulder finally ground to a halt, revealing a small, dark passageway into the mountain.

Whisker and Ruby rushed over and stepped inside, letting their eyes slowly adjust to the gloom. The tunnel continued into blackness. A scattering of broken rocks lay strewn across the floor, following the arc of the boulder.

'No wonder it was hard work,' Whisker said. 'From the look of these shards, we've been pushing a pile of rubble along.'

'Well, we're in now!' Ruby pointed out, brushing the rocks aside with her foot, 'so let's get going!'

'I wouldn't be in such a hurry, if I were you,' Mr Tribble called out. 'I'm not convinced that's the correct passage.'

'What?' Ruby gasped.

'We need to take a *right* tunnel,' Mr Tribble said. 'That one's on the left.'

'But there's only one tunnel,' Ruby frowned.

'Not necessarily,' Whisker said, examining the right side of the passage. 'There's a small gap between the boulder and the wall. I can see two larger rocks wedged in the gap. I think they're preventing the boulder from moving any further, but there appears to be hollow space on the other side of the wall.'

Rat Bait walked into the passage carrying a lit lantern and held it up to the gap.

'Ye be right,' he said. 'There's another passage b'yond.'

'Give me a hand with these rocks,' Whisker said.

Rat Bait put down the lantern and helped Whisker remove the first rock from the gap. No sooner had they pulled it free than the boulder jerked forward of its own accord. It stopped when it reached the second rock.

'Yikes!' Whisker cried, jumping back. 'Who's turning the wheel?'

Mr Tribble and Emmie held their empty paws in the air.

'It could be built-up tension,' Whisker considered. 'A

184

direct result of the boulder straining against the rubble. By removing the obstacles, the tension is being released, turning the door.'

'Ey?' Rat Bait said, scratching his chin.

Ruby rolled her eye. 'Aren't you the engineering expert, Whisker? Leverage, levers and all the rest … It pays to have an inventor for a father.'

'I, err, guess so,' Whisker said humbly. 'Circus inventions are far less complex than rotating boulders, but the principle's the same.'

'So can we release the tension by turning the wheel in the opposite direction?' Ruby asked.

'Trying – it – now,' Mr Tribble groaned. 'Sword – won't – budge.' He quickly gave up trying and slumped to the ground. 'I think this is a one-way-only kind of door.'

Whisker ran his paw over the boulder.

'The door is actually a carved piece of rock,' he said. 'From what I can see, it has three sides like a triangle. Two of them are flat and the third is curved. The curved side is currently facing us.'

'So from above it would look roughly like a slice of pie?' Ruby surmised.

'Exactly,' Whisker said, stepping outside the passage. He scratched a rough diagram on the ground with his sword.

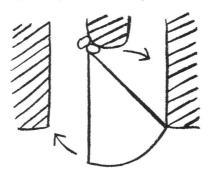

'Only one passage is accessible at a time,' he explained. 'As soon as the rubble is removed, the left passage will close and the right passage will open.'

'And there's no way of knowing if the left passage can be reopened,' Mr Tribble added. 'Or if it leads anywhere at all.'

'But the only way to remove the rocks is from inside,' Ruby said, 'and that would mean …'

'Saying goodbye to a scoundrel!' Rat Bait called from the passage.

Whisker looked up to see Rat Bait grabbing hold of the second rock.

'I never expected to leave this island alive,' Rat Bait muttered. 'Tell the Capt'n – tell 'im I did it for his crew.'

He lifted the rock. The mountain rumbled and the boulder spun on its axis.

'NO!' Whisker shouted, leaping forward in desperation.

Ruby grabbed Whisker's arm and pulled him back as the wedge of rock scraped past like an oversized millstone. Whisker watched helplessly as Rat Bait disappeared behind a wall of stone, his final words drifting through the narrowing gap. 'It's a fittin' destiny to be trapped in a treasure mountain, don't ye thi …'

THUD! With the echoing sound of stone hitting stone, the boulder came to a standstill. Rat Bait was gone and the right passage was wide open.

Whisker grasped the wheel and frantically tried to turn it – clockwise, anticlockwise, up and down. He beat it with his paws. He kicked it with his toes. It was no use. The wheel held fast.

He slumped to his knees in defeat, staring helplessly up at the wedge of rock blocking the left passage. Rat Bait was right in front of him, close enough to touch, yet trapped behind countless tons of immovable stone.

Whisker couldn't bring himself to look at the open passage. It didn't feel right. Despite all of Rat Bait's lies and deceit, Whisker knew he had ultimately made the biggest sacrifice: he had put the crew first, forsaking his own chance of survival. His actions were those of a noble captain, not a selfish scoundrel.

Loyalty before all else ... Whisker thought. *There was good in Rat Bait after all.*

Finding the strength, Whisker rose to his feet and gave the wheel a futile heave. He knew it was pointless, but there was nothing else he could do.

'Let it go,' Ruby said quietly. 'He made a choice.'

'A forced choice!' Whisker snapped, his frustration turning to anger. 'The Captain treated him like he was already dead.'

'How dare you judge my uncle!' Ruby hissed, prodding a finger into Whisker's chest. 'Rat Bait ruined his life and the life of my family. The Captain has a right to feel the way he does, don't you forget it!'

Whisker lowered his head. 'But it's not the way it's supposed to be. This island is for second chances.'

'Rat Bait got his second chance,' Ruby said firmly. 'And he did something good with it. Leave it at that.'

'I can't,' Whisker said, setting his jaw. 'I just can't.'

Ruby stared back at him and shook her head. 'Why must you insist on fixing everyone else's lives, Whisker?'

Whisker felt his anger boiling over.

'Because I can't fix my own!' he yelled.

He grabbed the remaining lantern and rushed into the tunnel before Ruby could see the tears filling his eyes.

TWENTY

The Right Turn

Ruby and the mice joined Whisker in the dark passage. There was no more talk of Rat Bait – or of Eaton. Their sole focus was the treasure and the twisting path that would lead them to it.

The passage appeared to be a continuous rock cave, its walls lined with long, hexagonal shaped rocks expanding upwards to form a jagged roof high above the silent party.

The strange block-like structure consisted mostly of basalt, a black volcanic rock with an occasional dark-green tinge. Whisker wondered if the entire island had once been a raging volcano with the circular ridge of the Treacherous Sea forming a giant volcanic mouth.

Many of the walls had images scratched into the rock with white, chalky stone. Some of the images resembled animals; others looked like primates or two-legged creatures called humans. There was no doubt they were drawn long before the treasure arrived on the island.

'I believe our mysterious mapmaker made use of pre-existing passages,' Mr Tribble said, studying the images. 'Inhabitants must have lived here long ago.'

'Let's hope they're not still around,' Ruby said warily. 'I've heard humans hate rodents more than cats!'

The companions pressed on uneasily until they reached a point where the tunnel split in two. Both passages rose steadily upwards. Steps were intermittently carved into the rocky ground.

'The symbol sheet says *left*,' Mr Tribble said. 'So we need to take the reverse passage, which of course is on the *right*.'

'Obviously,' Ruby muttered, already disappearing up the right stairs. 'Hurry up with that lantern.'

Obediently, Whisker followed after her.

The passage seemed to be an endless climb. It continued up and up and up with no sign of levelling off. Whisker began to wonder if they were suddenly going to pop out of the very top of the mountain.

The stairs finally opened out into a small chamber. Its walls were covered with small drawings of fish and bears. Three tunnels extended from the longest side of the musty space. Mr Tribble pointed to the central tunnel and the others followed him through.

The air grew damp as they continued, the heavy humidity making it difficult to breathe. Water droplets clung to the walls and the companions' clothes were cold and wet when they arrived at a rough set of stairs branching off from the left side of the tunnel.

Mr Tribble checked the symbols.

'Up we go,' he said.

They began to climb once again. Whisker knew that if Horace was with them, he'd be counting every step. But Horace wasn't with them, and the four companions had enough to concentrate on without idle chatter.

The stones beneath them became more perilously slippery with every step. The moss-covered walls provided

189

no handholds, and it was a struggle just to stay on two feet. The rodents reverted to a *four paws on the ground* approach, with Whisker carrying the lantern between his teeth.

Without warning, the stairs came to an abrupt end. Water seeped from a large rock in front of them, pooling at the top step and trickling over their toes.

'It's a dead-end!' Emmie squeaked.

'Mmmmmm,' Whisker responded.

Emmie screwed up her face in confusion. Whisker removed the lantern from his mouth and tried again.

'Up there,' he said. 'Between the rock and the ceiling. It looks like a narrow gap.'

'*Over the rock*,' Mr Tribble read from the sheet. 'The tunnel must continue through the gap.' He raised his head and added. 'If we can ever reach it …'

'Of course we can reach it,' Ruby said confidently. 'We've climbed Silver Falls, and that was three times as high!'

'But we only got halfway up,' Mr Tribble muttered.

Whisker tried not to think of their previous misadventure and hooked his tail around the handle of his lantern.

'Avoid the slimy, green patches,' he said, moving to the corner of the passage. 'I'd recommend climbing up the side of the rock where it joins the wall. There's a double set of paw-holds and far less water.'

Placing one foot on the wall and the other on the rock, Whisker began to scale the slippery surface. He concentrated as hard as he could on finding the right holds. It wasn't the fear of embarrassment that kept him from falling; it was the fear of breaking the only lantern and sending the passage into pitch-darkness.

After several tense minutes of calculated climbing, Whisker pushed off the last slippery foothold and reached the small gap above the rock. He dangled the lantern over the side so the others could see their way up to him.

Mr Tribble came next, his glasses fogging up. Emmie followed a safe distance behind, with Ruby gently coaxing her along. Ruby and Emmie had been cabin mates for several weeks and, although Ruby would never admit it, she seemed to enjoy being a big sister to the little mouse – when no one was watching.

Ruby joined the others at the top of the rock, flicking green spots of slime from her outfit. Slime was one thing Ruby did *not* enjoy.

'I'm afraid you're wasting your time, my dear,' Mr Tribble said politely. 'The next passage is riddled with moss and mould. It appears we're close to an underground water source.'

'A welcome bath,' Ruby groaned.

She got down on her paws and knees and crawled after Whisker through the low, wet passage. The sound of running water gurgled up ahead.

Whisker slid from the passage into a wide cavern. A shallow stream crossed the rocky floor, splitting the chamber in two. The occasional stalactite dangled from the ceiling like a giant out-of-place ice cream cone. The cavern had none of the grandeur of the thieves' cave on the Island of Kings, but the rushing water brought the entire chamber to life.

The golden rays of the lantern bounced off the rippling surface of the stream, scattering light over the broad roof of the cavern. The water flowed from right to left, gushing out of one wall and disappearing through a wide hole on the opposite side of the subterranean space. A narrow bank of rock on the far side of the cavern followed the stream in either direction.

'Where do we go from here?' Whisker asked.

'The next symbols stand for *water* and a *left passage*,' Mr Tribble said. 'It is my understanding that we need to cross the water and follow the passage upstream to the right.'

'I'm ready for my ice bath,' Ruby said, removing her swords. She held them above her head. 'The water looks shallow enough. Let's hope it's not strong enough to sweep us away.'

'Hang on, Ruby,' Whisker said, pulling her back. 'It's safer if we link arms and go across together.'

'Alright,' she reluctantly agreed, sticking her swords back in her belt. 'My swords are half rusted anyway.'

Whisker passed her the lantern.

'You go first with the lantern,' he said. 'The mice can follow you and I'll take up the rear.'

Ruby linked arms with Mr Tribble. Mr Tribble linked arms with Emmie. Emmie linked arms with Whisker and together the rodent-chain slipped into the icy water.

The current was strong but the water only rose as high as their waists. Emmie, the shortest of the party, was up to her neck. Her companions held on to her tightly, inching their way over the slippery rocks at the bottom of the stream. They crossed the stream without mishap and sloshed out on the opposite bank.

'I'm half clean, at least,' Ruby muttered, drying her swords on her vest.

'Let's keep moving before we catch a chill,' Mr Tribble said hastily.

Ruby passed Emmie the lantern. 'Here, hold it close and

you'll warm up in no time.'

'Th-th-thanks,' Emmie shivered.

The dripping companions followed the water upstream, walking single file along the narrow bank of rock, with Whisker leading the way. Although Emmie walked at the rear of the group with the lantern, there was enough light reflecting off the water for Whisker to see where he was going.

The stream led them through the wall of the cavern and along an echoing tunnel. The rocky bank became muddier as the companions went on and they had no choice but to squelch through large puddles alongside the stream. The tunnel widened, giving them enough room to walk two abreast.

Whisker could see the riverbank coming to an end further ahead. A solid wall of rock spanned the entire width of the tunnel. Water spurted from a hole in the wall, gushing out into a small pool. Whisker wondered if they had reached the very source of the mountain spring, the pure water meandering its way through the foothills and past the Rock of Hope to the sea.

To the left of the spring, a large rock archway framed two sets of crudely carved stairs. The right stairs ascended upwards through the wall. The left set of stairs twisted downwards.

'Right or left?' Whisker asked from a distance.

Mr Tribble adjusted his glasses and examined the symbols as he walked.

'Left stairs down,' he said hesitantly, 'though it appears we've missed a turn. There's a symbol here for a central passage with an arrow above it. I believe we have to go *up and over* a passage.'

'Brilliant,' Ruby scoffed. 'More climbing up ghastly green rocks!'

'Maybe there's something up there,' Whisker said, pointing to the top of the wall.

Ruby looked up, Mr Tribble kept his head buried in the symbol sheet and Whisker took another step forward. His foot never touched the ground.

He felt his stomach in his mouth as he fell through the air. Suddenly the lantern light was gone and everything was dark. He threw his arms above his head, grabbing desperately for a hold. His paw gripped something long and leg-like and the next moment he was sliding over slippery rocks and descending at pace with Ruby and Mr Tribble gasping beside him.

With a *SQUISH* and a *THUD*, the fall was over.

'Arrrr,' Whisker groaned, trying to sit up. 'What happened?'

'I think we found our missing passage,' Mr Tribble moaned. 'Or should I say *hole*?'

'I hardly call this *up and over*,' Ruby muttered, looking above her. 'It's more like down, down, down!'

'Where's Emmie?' Mr Tribble said frantically.

'I'm up here, silly!' Emmie shouted down. 'I was watching where *I* was going.'

Her three companions groaned in unison.

Whisker looked around at his surroundings. He was lying in shallow mud at the bottom of a deep hole. The wall on one side of the hole was slightly sloped. The opposite wall was dead straight and contained a deep alcove extending into the rock. The curved roof of the alcove was speckled with tiny blue lights, glowing like distant stars. Silk-like threads dangled beneath them.

'Glow worms!' Whisker exclaimed.

Mr Tribble picked up his glasses and positioned the muddy frames on his nose.

'*Arachnocampa* to be precise,' he said. 'They're technically not worms but the larvae stage of fungus gnats.'

Ruby rolled her eye. 'Oh joy. I'm surrounded by geniuses and look where it gets me: stuck in a muddy hole.'

'You fell in, too,' Whisker protested.

'Someone grabbed my leg!' Ruby hissed. '*Falling* is not the same as being *pulled*. Look it up, brainiac!'

'Yeah, yeah,' Whisker muttered.

'The question isn't how we got *in*, but how are we going to get *out*?' Mr Tribble said.

'You don't need the IQ of an owl to figure that out,' Ruby said, positioning herself against the sloped wall. 'We climb out, of course.'

She tried to pull herself up the smooth surface, grabbing whatever small divots in the rock she could find. One paw, two paw, slip – Ruby slid into the mud.

Angrily, she wiped the mud off her chin and tried again. One paw, one foot, *SPLAT* – Ruby tumbled down a second time.

'I'd offer you a boost,' Whisker said cautiously, 'but the hole is far too deep, even if we stood on each other's shoulders.' He looked up. 'Now if Emmie had a rope …'

'Well, she *doesn't* have a rope!' Ruby snapped. 'And a few strands of glow worm silk are hardly going to cut it. What we need is a *giant* worm to burrow through the ground and give us a free ride to the surface.'

'I wouldn't count on that happening in any hurry,' Mr Tribble said. 'The world's largest earthworm is …'

'Forget it,' Ruby groaned.

Mr Tribble forgot it and shut his mouth. Whisker didn't.

'What if we could get something *else* to push us to the surface?' he said.

'Like what?' Ruby asked, mid-frown.

'Listen,' Whisker said.

They all listened. The sound of the mountain spring gurgled above them.

'If Emmie can dig a trench in the mud and divert the water from the stream, we can float our way out!' Whisker exclaimed.

'And I'll finally get a proper bath,' Ruby sighed.

'Did you hear that, Emmaline, dear?' Mr Tribble called out.

'Yes, Mr Tribble,' Emmie squeaked back. 'You want me to fill the hole with water so Ruby can take a bath.'

'Something like that …' Mr Tribble muttered.

While Emmie scraped through the muddy ground, the three captives stared, mesmerised, at the small glow worm colony around them.

Whisker imagined he was lying on the top of the mountain, gazing up at the stars in search of new glow worm constellations. He spotted a candy cane galaxy, a watching eye and a bottle of milk. Ruby said the milk bottle was actually a bottle of blueberry juice. Whisker knew she had a thing for berries.

After a soothing session of star gazing, an icy trickle of water splashed over Whisker's shoulder, shocking his senses.

'Emmie the mighty mud mouse to the rescue!' cried a voice from above.

'Keep digging, *wonder paws!*' Ruby shouted back. 'We

196

need more than a trickle to fill this hole.'

'Don't worry!' Emmie said. 'I've built a dam.'

'A dam?' Mr Tribble echoed. 'Why did you build a dam? You're not a beaver. What we needed was a channel.'

'A dam is much better than a channel, silly!' Emmie squeaked. 'Ruby will get a shower *and* a bath. All I need to do is remove one flat rock and ...'

SPLASH!

A torrent of icy water hit Whisker from above, knocking him off his feet. He grabbed his pocket to stop the key washing away as the deluge filled the hole. In seconds he was rising upwards in a swirling blue mass of rodent limbs and glow worms.

Before Whisker or his shivering companions had a chance to give themselves a decent scrub, their saturated bodies popped out of the hole. Whisker grabbed a rock to stop himself from being swept into the stream and watched as the glow worms wriggled their way onto dry ground.

'Well done, Emmie!' Mr Tribble said, rising to his feet. 'That was invigorating, to say the least.'

Ruby coughed up a mouthful of water. 'A warning would have been nice ...'

Whisker patted Emmie on the head. 'Better than a beaver!'

Emmie gave him a proud smile.

'Let's keep moving,' Ruby said, straightening her water-logged vest. 'Lead the way, *water boy!*'

Whisker descended the stairs to the left, Emmie shuffled behind him with the lantern and the others kept pace, fixing their eyes firmly on every step. The stairs curved down in a wide spiral, leading the companions back in the direction they had come.

Tap, tap, tap ...

A faint sound drifted up the dark stairwell. Whisker's tail stood on end.

'Can you hear that?' he whispered.

'Sounds like footsteps,' Ruby murmured.

Whisker drew his sword and crept silently closer. He beckoned for Emmie to stay a few paces behind him, knowing he'd need all the room he could get to swing a sword in a cramped tunnel. Although he wasn't looking forward to running into a savage cave dweller, he was comforted by the fact that if something was down there, it wouldn't be much bigger than he was.

The stairs continued to curve downwards and Whisker was unable to see more than a few steps ahead. Nothing emerged from the shadows, but the sound continued.

Tap, tap, tap ...

The stairs levelled out and all of a sudden the sound was all around him.

TAP, TAP, CRACK, HISS ...

As Whisker watched in horror, hairline cracks appeared in the wall. Rocks vibrated, mud oozed from the ceiling and small jets of water spurted out of crevices.

It took Whisker a moment to figure out what was happening, but when he did, his entire body shuddered in terror. He was right under the flooded hole. The water was forcing its way out and the walls of the passage were about to burst.

The first rock blasted from the wall before Whisker could warn the others. Propelled by a powerful stream of water, it knocked Whisker's sword out of his paws and sent him sprawling to the ground.

The impact of the fall dislodged the map canister from

his belt and it rolled out of reach.

'RUN!' he shouted. 'UP THE STAIRS! GET OUT OF HERE!'

As Emmie turned to flee, a large rock exploded from the ceiling, crashing onto the passage floor behind her.

Emmie jumped clear and Whisker scrambled backwards on his elbows as an avalanche of water and rocks gushed through the hole, separating him from his companions.

He caught a final glimpse of his panicked friends dashing up the stairs, before the entire passage filled with rubble and he was swept away in a wave of inky blackness.

TWENTY-ONE

Alone

Whisker was alone. He was lying in a pool at the bottom of a passage with no sword, no lantern and no companions. But despite his predicament, he hadn't lost hope. He was within a twist and a turn of reaching the treasure and he still had the key.

Your friends are safe, he reassured himself. *You must go on.*

He stood up and looked around. The passage was dark, but it wasn't black. It was more of a greeny-blue colour. Whisker could just make out the shapes of steps rising out of the rippling water. Peering down at his reflection, he was startled to see his left shoulder glowing pale blue. He tilted his head and looked closer. A plump glow worm perched on the top of his shirt.

'Hello there,' Whisker said politely.

The glow worm began to fade.

'Wait, wait!' Whisker pleaded. 'Just hear me out.'

The glow worm brightened slightly.

'I'm, err … terribly sorry for flooding your home and all,' Whisker apologised, 'but if you could just keep glowing for a few more minutes, I'm sure I can find you a new home, with a much grander view. How does a treasure chamber sound?'

The glow worm wiggled and cranked its glow up to full strength.

'Much obliged,' Whisker said. 'Now let's find that treasure!'

Whisker and his new companion ascended the stairs. The passage curved left and then right, continuing to rise steadily before opening out into a small cave. The cave was roughly circular in shape and domed at the top. Its walls were smooth and blank with no markings and no signs of passages or doorways. The floor of the cave was a flat slab of rock.

Whisker removed the key from his pocket and held it in front of the glow worm. The mysterious symbols lit up like a stained glass window. Whisker studied the final two symbols: a clockwise turning arrow and a right paw.

'I need to find another wheel to turn,' he muttered.

The glow worm moved its head from side to side as if helping with the search.

Whisker moved into the centre of the cave and tapped his foot on the floor.

'I can't dig this time,' he said in agitation. 'The ground is solid rock.' He looked back at the entrance passage, perplexed. 'There's one way in and one way out ... or is there?'

He recalled something Mr Tribble had said on the opposite mountain.

'I may be *looking*,' Whisker thought aloud, 'but am I actually *seeing*?'

He considered the facts. 'I'm in a circular room. My instructions are to turn something clockwise. There is no wheel so what else is there?'

'Me!' he exclaimed.

He took another look at the symbols.

'The twisting arrow on the key appears to turn 270 degrees clockwise,' he considered. 'If I face the door and spin my body the required three-quarters of a revolution I end up – there!'

He pointed to a spot on the wall with his finger. Without taking his eyes off the wall, he hurried over and began rapping on the rock with his knuckles, searching for a hollow spot or a hidden lever. He reached up high, he bent down low, he banged and he kicked, but couldn't locate anything.

'Ok,' he said, catching his breath. 'Am I still missing something?'

'Of course!' he exclaimed, slapping himself in the forehead. 'The symbols need to be reversed. It's 270 degrees *anticlockwise.*'

Whisker returned to the centre of the room and repeated the process, turning the opposite direction. He walked over to the correct side of the wall and studied the rocks with his eyes.

In the light of the glow worm, he saw what he was looking for. An almost-invisible crack surrounded a small circle of rock halfway up the wall.

Brimming with excitement, Whisker placed both paws on the circle and pushed as hard as he could. The rock slowly moved into the wall.

Whisker heard a rumbling sound and looked over his shoulder. The walls and the floor of the cave were motionless. He kept pushing and the grinding sound continued.

He looked again, this time directing his eyes beyond the cave to the passage through which he had entered. A rough rock door swung open in the wall near the top step.

Clever move, Whisker thought. *No one would think to look there.*

The door ground to a halt, fully open. Whisker removed his paws from the circle of stone. The door immediately began to close.

'Drat!' Whisker cried, jumping back from the wall.

The door appeared to be closing quicker than it had opened. Whisker spun on his heel and sprinted from the cave. Without giving it a second thought, he took a flying leap and threw himself through the narrow gap – barely scraping through.

With an echoing *THUD* … D… D… the door slammed behind him, the rumbling echo of the door reverberating through the stones of the mountain.

Whisker stood up and checked on the health of his passenger. The glow worm flickered on and off several times before resuming its steady glow.

Relieved he hadn't caused any permanent light-damage to the little creature, Whisker felt the sides of the door, searching for a release lever or another stone button. He found nothing – he was a captive in the treasure chamber.

It took Whisker a moment to slow his pounding heart as the reality of the situation sank in. Trying to remain calm, he turned his back on the door and slowly looked around him.

In the pale blue light, he made out a long wall stretching to his left. To his right, he saw nothing but blackness. Curious, he took a step closer and realised he was standing on the edge of a deep precipice. The faint sound of running water far below told him it was a long way to fall.

He pulled himself away from the edge and moved to the safety of the wall, running his eye along its rough surface. Several paces ahead of him, a dark shape jutted out of the rock.

Could it be? he thought excitedly.

He tiptoed along the wall. The echo of the stone door still rang in his ears, but his mind was focused on one thing: the object in front of him.

He drew closer and the shape became clearer. It had semi-circular sides and a curved top. Its surface resembled rusted metal. Whisker reached the strange object and realised it was the lid of a mighty chest, built into the stone wall of the cavern. In the centre of the lid was a small keyhole.

A myriad of thoughts, feelings and memories surged through Whisker's mind. His tail danced in delight. He had done it. He had located the fabled treasure. One turn of the key and the treasure would be his, his destiny would be defined – his questions would be answered. He almost imagined his parents and sister jumping out of the chest the moment he opened it. He would finally have his life back. There would be no more fighting, no more narrow escapes and no more cats.

He removed the key from his pocket, moving closer to the chest – and stopped. Something held him back. It wasn't doubt, or uncertainty, or even fear – it was the rumbling sound in his ears.

Echoes don't last that long, he thought.

The sound grew louder and clearer. Whisker looked further along the wall to where a huge stone archway stood at the end of the chamber. A deep growling sound resonated from the blackness beyond and with it came the terrible stench of rotting fish. Whisker knew he wasn't alone.

He raised his startled eyes to the top of the archway. Carved into the uppermost stone was the symbol of a paw. It wasn't the right paw of royalty; it was the left paw of the great brown bear.

Whisker's tail froze in fear. The rest of his body didn't. Frantically, he wedged the King's Key into the keyhole.

My only place to hide, he thought desperately.

The key slid past the first tooth and stopped.

'What?' he gasped.

He tried jiggling the key. It didn't move. By now, the growls of the bear had risen to a volume that rivalled thunder.

Whisker removed the key and peered into the hole. A small shard of stone lay wedged beneath the surface. He tried to prise it out with his finger but the rock stuck fast.

The growling suddenly stopped and Whisker looked up. The huge furry shape of a bear filled the archway, its broad shoulders almost touching the stones on either side. It sniffed the air and tilted its head to face the terrified treasure thief.

Whisker knew the time to hide had come and gone – the bear had caught his scent.

'Cursed onions!' he hissed under his breath.

The bear lowered itself onto all fours and cautiously crept towards Whisker, continuing to sniff the dank air of the cavern. Whisker slipped the key into his pocket and inched away from the metal lid.

'I-I-I w-w-was just leaving, Mr Bear,' he stammered.

'S-s-see, y-y-your treasure is still h-h-here. I haven't t-t-touched a thing. I s-s-swear.'

The bear either couldn't understand his language or took offense to Whisker's stammering excuses. It raised itself onto two powerful legs and, bearing its huge canine teeth, let out an almighty *GRRRR!*

Whisker was sprayed with fishy slobber.

'AAAAAR!' he cried as the bear slashed his claws through the air.

The brown beast advanced, taking wild swipes at the petrified rat. Whisker stumbled back, struggling to stay out of paw's reach.

He tried to imagine the bear as a giant koala, in need of a friendly hug, but the positive thinking didn't work. The bear drew closer, one growling step at a time, herding Whisker into a corner.

With a desperate look over his shoulder, Whisker realised he had nowhere to go. There was a solid wall to his left, a sheer drop to his right, a door that wouldn't open behind him and the biggest of all bears towering above him. The only thing Whisker had in his favour was his size. He kept his small frame low to the ground and the bear's powerful paws swept harmlessly over the back of his head.

The bear was a quick learner. It abandoned *swiping* and turned to *thumping*. Hammer-like blows pounded the ground around Whisker. He frantically darted and weaved between huge paws, escaping crushing blows by mere millimetres.

Fear fuelled his mind and he knew he must act quickly if he was ever going to survive.

Good offense is the best defence, he recalled. *You must*

attack.

With the bear's next blow, Whisker scurried to the very edge of the precipice. The bear took a step to its left, spreading its legs, and raised its paw for the knock-out blow.

Whisker seized his opportunity and charged at the bear. He didn't need a weapon; all he needed was size and speed. Before the bear knew what was happening, Whisker had squeezed his tiny body between its legs and was racing along the wall towards the giant archway.

The bear roared in fury as Whisker bounded through the archway and sprinted down a rough passage, with the glow worm clinging on for dear life.

There's got to be another way out, he thought, increasing his pace.

He came to a fork in the passage. A steep tunnel descended sharply to the left, the other rose gently to the right. There were no markings to indicate which direction he should take.

Whisker took a guess and chose right. He took one step into the tunnel and stopped. Directly ahead of him, the tunnel divided into three.

'We're about to get hopelessly lost,' he groaned.

He could hear the bear on his tail and knew he had to keep moving. He also needed to find his way back to the treasure.

'The pencil lead!' he gasped.

He reached into his bag and pulled out Pete's broken red lead. It was stuck to something squishy and smelly: Fred's mouldy cheese.

No wonder the bear can smell me, he thought.

He drew a rough arrow on the wall with the lead, then

unwrapped the cheese from its cloth and hurled it down the left tunnel. Hoping the bear would take his bait, he sprinted up the right tunnel to where the passage split into three.

He caught a waft of the foul fish smell from the centre passage and followed it through, marking the wall with the lead as he went.

The fish had to get in here somehow, he reasoned. *Maybe the smell will lead me out of the mountain?*

The sound of the bear grew fainter as he continued. Whisker knew his own onion odour would at least be masked by the fishy smell, which seemed to be growing worse by the minute.

He followed several more passages and stumbled into a small cave, its floor littered with a pile of dried bones, decomposing fish heads and the bodies of half-chewed salmon.

'The bear's lair,' Whisker mumbled in horror, covering his mouth to block the atrocious smell.

He frantically scanned the walls of the cave, hoping to discover a passage to the outside world. The walls were a seamless curve of solid rock. There were no visible openings and no narrow cracks to squeeze through. It was clear he had reached a dead end.

He turned to leave, hoping another tunnel would lead him out of the mountain, when a large growl rumbled down the passage.

Whisker's fur stood on end, his tail twisted into a knot. The bear was right outside the cave and he was trapped.

Salmon Stew

Whisker stared at the rotting carcasses of salmon, trout and other unfortunate river dwellers strewn across the floor. Eyeballs stared back at him, dead, cold, expressionless. Whisker knew he might soon be joining them. He could take his last stand as a noble warrior and face the bear with his paws raised and head held high … *or* …

A desperate idea entered Whisker's head. No self-respecting warrior would even consider it, but Whisker wasn't a warrior, he was a Pie Rat and Pie Rats did things the sneaky way.

Whispering 'lights out,' to the glow worm, he grabbed his nose and dived, headfirst, into the salmon stew.

He wriggled his body under a fin, stuck his foot in an open mouth and covered his head and shoulders with dried scales. The light of the glow worm dimmed and Whisker laid perfectly still, waiting in utter darkness.

The bear entered the room, shuffling slowly over the stones, its huge, black nose sniffing the air.

CRUNCH! With a casual step to its right, it crushed a salmon skull with its paw.

Whisker tried not to squirm, desperately hoping *his*

skull wasn't next.

The bear stepped further into the pile of fish scraps, examining a salmon head near Whisker's tail.

Don't twitch, Whisker silently pleaded. *Don't move …*

His tail, for once, stayed as still as a cobra in a coma.

The bear lingered near him a moment longer, then, taking one last look at its horrid horde, let out an annoyed grunt and headed out of the cave.

Whisker remained motionless, listening to the sounds of the bear descending a side tunnel. He waited until the scuffles and growls had faded completely and dragged himself from the rotting heap.

'What is it with me and bad smells?' he muttered, plucking a salmon scale from his black bandanna.

The glow worm responded by switching itself on again.

Whisker tiptoed from the cave, continuing along the passage, until he reached the side tunnel the bear had taken. For a moment, he considered following it down – on the off chance it would lead him to freedom – but in the end, he decided that pursuing his pursuer was hardly the wisest of moves and opted to take the next tunnel instead.

Only metres into the tunnel, Whisker heard a distant grinding sound and a familiar *THUD … D … D …*

His eyes grew wide. His heart beat increased.

Ruby's in the treasure chamber, he thought. *She's found a way through!*

Overjoyed, he hurried from the tunnel and raced back the way he had come, following the red arrows on the walls. Right, left, centre, down … He moved silently and swiftly.

He passed the final fork in the passage to see warm light streaming from the chamber ahead and increased his pace. *They're waiting for me.*

He burst through the stone archway, puffing hard, and continued running until he reached a small candle perched on top of the chest. He stopped and looked around. No one was there.

'Ruby?' he whispered, suddenly growing anxious. 'Mr Tribble? Emmie?'

He heard a soft footfall behind him and spun around. Out of the shadows of the archway stepped the foreboding silhouette of Captain Sabre.

'Sorry to disappoint you,' he purred maliciously, 'but your friends are rather tied up at present.'

Whisker felt a surge of panic run through his tail.

'R-Ruby doesn't get *tied up*,' he stammered in disbelief.

'Come now,' Sabre said, stepping into the candlelight. 'Let's not blame the poor girl. It's hardly *her* fault a large net landed on her head. If we're going to blame anyone it might as well be you, young apprentice.' He chuckled to himself. 'You left quite a trail for Prowler to follow, not to mention all the secrets you kindly revealed. The wind carries every whisper on this island.' He waved his paw theatrically through the air.

A deep frown ran across Whisker's forehead.

'Why the sour face?' Sabre asked mockingly. 'Your worthless rodent buddies are just behind the door. You can join them if you like – just hand me the key.'

'Y-you're lying,' Whisker said, fighting for confidence. 'Y-you're stuck in here just like me.'

Sabre glared at him, his patience dwindling. 'Unlike your snivelling friends, Cat Fish stick together. My crew are just outside, awaiting my next order. Two taps on the door and your little girlfriend gets it. Three taps on the door and *open sesame*, the door swings open and everyone goes free.'

Whisker knew Sabre couldn't be trusted. His instinct told him that as soon as the Cat Fish captain had the key, he'd give the execution order.

But what other choice do I have? Whisker asked himself. *A frantic dash for the door? Sabre will surely cut me down before I can even knock ... I need more options – I need a plan.*

'My key,' Sabre hissed. 'Hand it over now, or there'll be consequences.'

Whisker didn't respond. He took a deep breath, calming his anxious mind and willed his memories to find him an answer – like they always did. But as hard as he tried, nothing came to him. No clever sword move. No flying pie manoeuvre. No circus stunt.

Sabre stepped forward, his paw outstretched. 'Make the right choice, apprentice.'

Whisker felt his own paw drawn to the key like it was a magnet. He resisted the compelling urge to give in and pulled his paw away.

This isn't how it ends, he told himself. *You have to find a way. Clear your head. Think!*

Sabre extended his claws, greedily awaiting his prize. Whisker remained motionless, his eyes glazing over as if hypnotised by the soft gurgle of the mountain stream.

'There's no rescue party for you this time,' Sabre sneered over the sound of the water. 'I hardly think your pathetic pie ship can sail up an underground river, do you?'

Whisker knew Sabre was right – the *Apple Pie* wasn't coming to save him, but that didn't mean he was alone. Among the gentle sounds of running water, Whisker heard a faint growl. It filled him with terror – and with hope. The monster of the mountain was now Whisker's greatest ally.

Sabre continued staring at him, oblivious to the sounds of the bear. Whisker took a quick step towards the precipice, aware that the Cat Fish captain would hear the growls soon enough.

'Give me the key!' Sabre snarled, taking an air swing at Whisker.

Whisker jumped back, landing awkwardly on one foot, his left heel balanced precariously on the very edge of the precipice.

Steadying himself, he pulled the key from his bag and slowly raised his arm over the dark expanse. He'd practiced his routine on the cliff top. It was time for him to perfect it in the cavern.

'Haven't we already been through this?' Sabre hissed.

With a wicked gleam in his eye, Whisker extended his arm further over the edge.

'New round, new rules!' he shouted, his voice bouncing off the walls of the cave. 'Now stay back.'

Sabre held his ground. 'You won't drop it,' he smirked, confidently. 'You care too much for your friends.'

'And you care too much for the treasure,' Whisker shot back.

Sabre lurched forward, impulsively grabbing for Whisker's arm. Whisker flinched, pretending to drop the key.

Sabre froze. A look of panic ran across his face.

'BACK!' Whisker cried. 'I'm warning you.'

Sabre snarled in rage. 'Drop it and I'll tap twice! Do you hear?'

Whisker heard the low grunts of the bear approaching

and knew his rescue was close at hand.

'I'M NO FOOL!' he yelled at the top of his lungs, drowning the sounds of the bear. 'Haven't you heard of the Pie Rat code? *Your brother is a rat, but don't trust a cat!* I follow the rules, Sabre, and the rules say you can't be trusted. You won't release Ruby, you won't release the mice, so there's no way you're getting this key!'

Before Sabre could respond, Whisker swung his arm over his shoulder and hurled the key across the cavern. Sabre watched in horror as the key sped through the air, bounced over the stone floor and skidded to a halt in the centre of the archway. It took Sabre a moment to realise the key *hadn't* gone over the precipice.

Whisker flashed Sabre an exaggerated look of disappointment – just to be sure. Sabre gave Whisker a vicious smile and leapt after the key.

'Lucky me!' he purred.

Without a word, Whisker turned and fled in the opposite direction.

He was only halfway to the door when he heard a deafening roar behind him. He looked over his shoulder to see Sabre scooping up the key as the mighty bear burst through the archway.

The bear battered Sabre aside like a rag doll, sending the key flying out of his paws. The key ricocheted off the archway and disappeared over the edge of the precipice. Sabre hissed in anger. The bear roared in fury and charged after Whisker.

Fuelled by fear, Whisker ran like the wind. Driven by rage, the bear ran like the wind on *'windy, windy island'* and reached Whisker in seconds.

With the door right in front of him, Whisker skidded

to a halt and threw himself to the ground. Unable to stop, the bear bounded over him, and collided with the stone door with a hard *THUD!*

Reeling in anger, it staggered back and slammed the door with its paw.

THUD!

'Two taps!' Whisker gasped.

He leapt to his feet and pushed his way through the matted jungle of brown fur above him. The bear looked down in rage and took a wild swipe at the tiny creature.

Whisker felt the powerful palm of the bear strike his torso, knocking the wind out of his lungs. His body flew backwards and crashed into the centre of the door.

THUD!

Whisker slid down the stone and dropped to the ground in a crumpled heap. He peered up through bleary eyes to see the bear standing over him and hoped Sabre had been telling the truth about one thing – *three knocks and the door opens.*

The bear opened its jaws and let out a savage ROAR! At the same moment, the door began to move. Bright light streamed through the widening gap, dazzling the startled bear.

Whisker rolled free from the path of the door as four bound bodies tumbled through. He felt a wave of relief pass through him – Ruby and the mice were alive.

The twins, tied back-to-back, struggled to stay upright and crashed to the ground. Mr Tribble, arms tightly bound behind him, tripped over the mice and nose-planted into the belly of the bear. His glasses spun off his nose and landed against the wall.

The bear lumbered forward, regaining its senses, and

flung Mr Tribble backwards into Ruby. Ruby, in the process of wriggling one arm free, managed to stay on her feet and staggered out of the bear's path.

The great brute stared through the open doorway at the terrified faces of Prowler and Furious Fur, unsure of who or what to attack next.

The door began to close and the bear stepped forward.

Prowler grabbed Eaton's lantern from a rock and shone it directly into the bear's face. It covered its eyes with its paws and blindly stumbled backwards.

Seizing his opportunity, Whisker darted across the cavern to help the twins. Before he could reach them, an orange and black body barged him out of the way. Whisker raised his arms in defence, but a wayward kick sent him tumbling to the ground. Helplessly, he watched as Captain Sabre hurdled over the mice and leapt through the door.

The light disappeared and with a *THUD* ... *D* ... *D* ... the door slammed shut, leaving Whisker and his companions trapped with the bear.

The manic beast reached down and scooped up the terrified twins in its arms. The mice squealed in terror. Without a weapon, Whisker did the only thing he could think of and leapt onto the foot of the bear, sinking his front teeth into its toes.

The bear howled in pain, dropping the mice onto the rocky floor of the cavern. With a sharp flick of its foot, it dislodged Whisker from its toes and took a follow-up swing at him with its right paw.

Whisker ducked out of the way, but the bear's claw caught a strand of rope dangling from Ruby's arm. She was flung off her feet and soared towards the precipice.

With one arm free, she managed to grab a rock as she bounced over the edge. Her body swung like a pendulum. Whisker saw her fingers slipping.

Ignoring the bear, he took a running step forward and flung himself towards the edge. His right paw caught Ruby's arm as her fingers released their grip. She was secure, but Whisker's body kept moving.

With a sudden feeling of déjà vu, he whipped his tail behind him, coiling it around a rock. As his tail took the strain, he threw his left paw over his shoulder and gripped the edge of the cliff.

Everything stopped moving. Whisker hung twisted at the top of the precipice, with Ruby clinging to his arm.

'Hold on,' he gasped. 'Just hold on.' He wished desperately it was that simple.

He looked down at Ruby, struggling to maintain her grip on his paw, and felt the bear's breath on the back of his neck.

Ruby stared back at him with a terrified expression on her face and whispered, 'Let go. Save yourself.'

In that instant, a dozen emotions raced through Whisker's mind: fear, despair, love ... regret – He knew he had no choice. There was only one decision he could live – or die – with.

Tightening his grip on Ruby's arm, he waited for the end.

TWENTY-THREE

Angels

A bright light appeared from the roof above Whisker, illuminating everything in its path. It wasn't lantern light – it was heavenly light, pure and clear. Whisker stared in wonder as the girl on the end of his arm transformed into a scarlet angel, her face a radiant vision of warmth and beauty.

Am I dead? he thought. *Is this rat heaven?*

His ears suddenly filled with the sound of falling rocks and the startled squeaks of the mice. The next moment, a huge hairy shadow passed over his head, disappearing into the darkness. A splash echoed from far below, followed by the defeated cries of the bear.

The sounds slowly faded. The stream gurgled softly, washing all of Whisker's fears away. Wearily, he pulled himself onto the cliff top, hauling Ruby with him. It was exhausting work. His arms ached. His scarlet angel had no wings.

He crouched on the edge of the precipice, his muscles burning, his lungs gasping for air. He wasn't in heaven, but the dazzling light around him told him heaven was close enough to touch.

As Whisker's eyes adjusted to the heavenly aura, Ruby

freed her second arm from the rope and gave him a look that was anything but angelic.

'You're as foolish as you are reckless, Whisker,' she snapped, unable to hide her trembling voice. 'You had one chance of survival. Why didn't you take it?'

Whisker interpreted Ruby's gruff address as her way of saying *thanks for saving me*.

'I guess there's *more to life than survival*,' he said sheepishly. 'It's something the Hermit taught me.' He paused and added, 'And some rats are really hard to let go.'

Ruby's face softened. She looked at Whisker and smiled. It wasn't an angelic smile, it was something much better: it was a rare *Ruby* smile.

'You're lucky your *one* chance of survival turned into *two*,' she said. 'We're both lucky.'

Whisker knew it was more than luck. He looked across at the pile of rocks in the centre of the floor. Lying unconscious on the top of the heap and gently snoring in the sunlight was the *real* angel of the mountain – Rat Bait.

'I guess he found a way out,' Whisker said.

'Or a way in,' Ruby added, pointing to the ceiling. 'There's a tunnel right above us that appears to lead straight out of the mountain.'

'It's a pity we didn't know that from the start,' Mr Tribble muttered, sitting up. 'It would have saved us a great deal of bother.' He sniffed the air. 'I take it the bear has gone? I can't see a thing without my glasses.'

'I think he went swimming,' Whisker murmured.

'Is that why I can smell fish?' Mr Tribble asked.

'Err, no ... that would be me,' Whisker sighed.

'You're glowing, too!' Mr Tribble exclaimed. 'Has the treasure transformed you into a deep-sea phosphorescent fish?'

Ruby rolled her eye and began untying the twins. Whisker picked up Mr Tribble's spectacles from the floor and positioned them on his nose.

'Now I see!' Mr Tribble exclaimed. 'It's an *Arachnocampa* fungus gnat.'

The glow worm dulled slightly.

'I think he prefers *glow worm*,' Whisker said. 'And no, I didn't get a chance to open the chest. I was too busy …'

SCRRRRRR … The door began to open.

'Here we go again,' Whisker muttered.

'A second bear would be handy right about now,' Ruby scowled, grabbing Rat Bait's sword and moving towards the entrance.

Whisker picked up a shard of stone and stood by her side as light streamed through the open doorway, heralding an onslaught of armed attackers. They flooded in with a *SQUEAK* and a *BUZZ*.

'AVAST YE SCURVY SARDINES!' cried an over-excited voice.

'Put up your paws!' roared another.

'Onions ahoy!' cheered a third.

'I'll flatten you like a fritter!' boomed a fourth.

'I can't see any bears, Captain?' sniffled a fifth.

The excitement quickly fizzled out.

Whisker dropped his stone, Ruby lowered her sword and their beloved Captain Black Rat gave them a formal salute.

'Crew at ease,' he said, jovially. 'It appears everyone is alive and well.'

'Only just,' Mr Tribble muttered.

'Cheer up, Tribble,' Horace laughed. 'The gallant heroes have arrived to rescue you.'

'Rescue us from what?' Ruby scoffed. 'A glow worm? You're a bit late for the real battle.'

Horace pointed a hot chilli sauce bottle at her. 'Rotten pies to you, too, Ruby! We've just fought an entire crew of Cat Fish to get here. And we retrieved your swords from a flooded tunnel. A little gratitude wouldn't go astray.'

'Technically, we only fought two Cat Fish,' Pete muttered. 'Furious Fur was asleep on a rock and the others ran in the opposite direction yelling *Bear! Bear!*'

'Well, they might come back,' Horace said defensively. 'And then you'll need us.'

'I doubt they'll return,' Whisker said, as Fred handed him a slightly bent green scissor sword, 'not without a key.'

'W-what happened to the key?' Horace gasped.

'The bear knocked it out of Sabre's paw,' Whisker explained.

'So where is it now?' Horace asked, staring around the cavern.

Whisker pointed over the edge of the precipice.

'Oh dear,' Fred groaned. 'Oh double dear.'

'Rotten pies to King's Keys,' Horace moped. 'If only I had my skeleton key.'

'Well you don't!' Pete snorted. So stop your whining. It's your fault you're as clumsy as Whisker and lost your stupid skeleton key on Prison Island.'

'But Madam Pearl promised to buy me a new one!' Horace grumbled.

'Well she can't buy it now, can she?' Pete snapped. 'She's stuck in the next room with a paw on a button and I haven't seen a single locksmith, keysmith or burglar supply shop on this entire stinking island!'

'Ahem,' Whisker interrupted, his face breaking into a sly grin.

Pete and Horace stopped arguing and turned to look at him. Whisker reached into his right pocket and pulled something out. The Hermit's eyes lit up.

'Ratbeard's reward!' the Captain exclaimed.

'Hey!' Horace cried. 'Isn't that …?'

'Yep,' Whisker said, giving the Hermit a grateful smile. 'The one and only.'

'Pays to have a copy,' the Hermit chuckled. 'Just in case.'

Whisker handed him the King's Key – not the rusty metal copy from the Hermit's bag that vanished over the edge – but the *real* King's Key.

'You started this quest,' he said. 'You deserve the honour of finishing it.'

The Hermit took the key and bowed. 'Honour belongs to Hermit, yes, yes, but treasure belongs to everyone.'

'Oh, one last thing,' Whisker said. 'There's a small rock stuck in the keyhole. We might need something sharp like –'

'– a hook to get it out!' Horace cried, rushing over to the chest. 'Better than any skeleton key!'

While Horace fiddled with the keyhole, Ruby and Pete untied the mice and Fred wedged his fighting fork in the door to stop it closing. Madam Pearl joined the others around the chest. The moment had finally come.

With all the fleeing and fighting and searching and surviving, Whisker hadn't had time to prepare himself for what he was about to discover. His hopes were high and his tail tingled as the Hermit inserted the key.

Click. One simple turn and the lid unlocked.

The Pie Rats positioned themselves around the huge metal lid and collectively heaved. It took all their strength to raise it off the rock. A waft of stale air drifted through the gap and with it came a familiar smell – the smell of Pete's cabin.

The lid swung back against the wall and the Pie Rats peered inside. At the bottom of a shallow pit lay a single dust-covered book. The Hermit carefully lifted the book and handed it to Whisker.

'Our treasure,' he whispered.

Whisker took the book in his paws and studied it closely. It was extremely thick and felt even heavier than it looked. Its embossed cover was bound in a finely woven fabric and coated in a dense resin. The edges of its pages were whiter than any book Whisker had ever seen and he wondered if it had ever seen the light of day.

Despite its mysterious grandeur, the book was still a book, and Whisker had hoped for something more: *a crystal ball … a magic staff … an item of great power?* He'd tried to convince himself that such magical items could exist. He wanted to believe in miracles, that anything was possible. But staring down at the cover of the book, all he felt was bitter disappointment. He was like a birthday boy unwrapping a gift he wished was something else.

Still, he told himself, *a book is better than nothing at all.*

He put on a brave face and clung to a faint hope that the book contained the answer he'd been waiting for – *where is my family?*

With the rest of the crew watching him closely, Whisker brushed a layer of dust off the cover, revealing several lines of flaked gold writing.

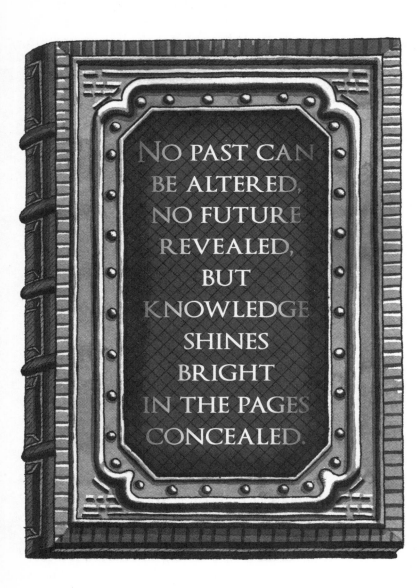

NO PAST CAN
BE ALTERED,
NO FUTURE
REVEALED,
BUT
KNOWLEDGE
SHINES
BRIGHT
IN THE PAGES
CONCEALED.

'More blasted riddles,' Pete mumbled, pointing to the words. 'I'm all for books, don't get me wrong, but a ton of diamonds wouldn't go astray.'

Without a response, Whisker placed his finger on the corner of the cover and flipped the book open.

The first page was blank.

Whisker turned to the second page. It was blank, too.

The third page – blank.

The fourth – blank.

He flicked through the pages with his thumb. Blank, blank, blank, blank, blank, blank, blank ... Every page was the same: blank.

In stunned silence, Whisker closed the cover and reread the golden riddle ... *knowledge shines bright in the pages concealed.*

He opened the book one last time. The pages were as white as sun shining on snow, but there was no knowledge, no wisdom, no power – no answers. The book was a blank journal, a sketchbook, whatever he wanted it to be.

Whisker wanted it gone.

He felt rage boiling up inside of him. He gritted his teeth. 'All of this for a blank book?'

'It's ironic really ...' Pete began.

'IT'S NOT IRONIC!' Whisker exploded, hurling the book at the pile of rocks. 'It's a sick joke.'

The book hit the ground, bursting open. Whisker shook his fist at the open book like it was a living creature.

'I believed in you!' he yelled. 'I trusted you. I did what you asked. I solved your riddles. I defeated your guardians ... and-and you gave me – nothing!'

He slumped to his knees and covered his face with his paws. The crew watched, bewildered.

'You were supposed to find them,' he sobbed. 'You were supposed to bring them back. You were supposed to fix everything ...' His voice trailed off.

No one spoke. The glow worm dimmed. Through the pained silence, Whisker felt the eyes of the entire crew staring at him, judging him, seeing him for what he really was: nothing more than a pathetic dreamer. He drew a deep breath and exhaled, releasing what anger he had left.

'I'm such an idiot,' he muttered. 'It was a stupid hope, I know.'

'It wasn't stupid,' Horace said quietly, placing his paw on Whisker's shoulder. 'Believe me, I should know. I'm the king of stupid.'

Pete snorted.

Horace waved his hook in Pete's general direction and continued, 'Most rats would have given up hope of finding their family the day of the cyclone, but not you, Whisker. You're more than a survivor. You're an inspiration.'

'Hear, hear!' Fred concurred.

'Whisker slowly looked up. Fred's giant face grew even wider with a beaming smile. The Captain nodded in admiration and Ruby, tough as nails Ruby, pretended she had something in her teary eye.

'You don't need a magical treasure to find your family,' Horace went on, 'you've got everything it takes: courage, determination, ingenuity, not to mention boatloads of luck – and that's just a start! I could go on and on all day, but that would be rambling, so I'll leave it at that before Pete calls us both nasty names –'

Horace shut his mouth and Whisker felt slightly less stupid. Pete stamped his pencil leg in annoyance.

'Why am I always the bad guy?' he snapped. 'I had no

intention of calling our fragile young apprentice *stupid, dim-witted* or *a cry baby.* He's clearly worked up about the book. *I'm* worked up about the book! We're broke, half-dead, fishy-smelling, and all we have to show for it is a choose-your-own adventure book with no beginning, no middle and no end!'

Smudge joined the conversation with an aerobatic circle around Pete's head.

'Buzz off!' Pete hissed. 'Can't you see I'm busy being miserable!'

Smudge pointed four arms frantically at the book as if to say *the misery can wait!*

All eyes turned to the open book. A ray of warm sunlight crept across one of its pages. Where the light hit, numbers and letters began to form.

The Pie Rats gasped in amazement as the sunlight brought the empty page to life.

The book wasn't blank after all.

The Book of Knowledge

In amazement, Horace stepped closer to the open book.

'Stay back! Don't touch it!' Pete barked. 'We don't know what it is.'

'Sun-reactive ink,' Mr Tribble gasped. *'Knowledge shines bright in the pages concealed …* it's a stroke of genius!'

'And it's perfectly harmless,' Madam Pearl added. 'I had a few letters written in a similar ink pass through my antiques shop a few years back. They were written by an explorer. He never signed his name.'

Using the tip of his hook, Horace slid the book across the floor until it was fully bathed in sunlight. Two entire pages filled with text.

Whisker's heart leapt as he stared at the words.

'Medicine for my misery!' Pete exclaimed.

'What is it?' Fred asked. 'Not all of us can read, you know.'

Pete screwed up his nose. 'This, you big buffoon, is the original recipe for my famous Pie Rat healing medicine.'

Mr Tribble adjusted his glasses. 'According to these quantities, you've been using too many of the eyeball-looking herbs, Pete.'

'Creative license,' Pete muttered. 'Just like the three sets of waves on your map.'

'Hey!' Fred said excitedly. 'Do you think there are any *pie* recipes in there?'

'There's only one way to find out!' Horace said, flicking to another page.

The sun bathed the surface of the paper and the outline of a map slowly appeared, followed by an ocean dotted with islands.

'The Cyclone Sea!' the Captain marvelled. 'And it's filled with uncharted islands we never knew existed.' He pointed to the map. 'Here is the Island of Destiny, and look, to the west, there are three islands, close to where we found Whisker.'

'You don't think my family could be ...?' Whisker gasped.

'There's a good chance,' Horace said. 'We can sail past the islands on the way home.'

Whisker couldn't believe what he was hearing, what he was seeing. The book had brought him a new hope. If his family were out there, he had the perfect tool to find them.

As the pages were turned, wondrous things flashed before his eyes: locations of unseen reefs; designs of fantastic inventions; references to lost treasure and sunken ships; charts showing wind directions and ocean currents; pages of chemical formulae; scientific principles; historical sea battles won and lost; ambush and defence strategies; and there were maps – dozens and dozens of maps.

'Now that I think of it, the riddle on the cover makes perfect sense,' the Captain said. 'This book won't change our past, nor will it tell us our future, but it will influence our destiny. The knowledge contained here could make us the most powerful crew on the seven seas.'

'If we all learnt to read,' Pete scoffed.

'Whoever wrote these words clearly had an infatuation with light,' Mr Tribble said. 'We first saw it with the map, then the key and now the book.'

'Turn to the front page,' Pete said, pushing in front of Horace. It might tell us who the author is.'

Pete used his bony fingers to flick the pages to the beginning. The title page drifted into view:

The complete discoveries
of

ADMIRAL AUGUSTUS 'ANSO' WINTERBOTTOM

Explorer, Discoverer and Adventurer

'Flaming flamingos!' Horace exclaimed. 'It's Whisker's great-grandfather, Anso.'

Dumbfounded, Whisker took a second look at the title page. He couldn't believe what he was seeing, and yet all of a sudden it made perfect sense. He'd been following the trail of his great-grandfather the whole time. Anso's advice, passed down through his father, had helped him solve riddles, defeat guardians and had saved him time and time again.

It took Whisker a few moments for it all to sink in. The book gave him more than just advice; it gave him his great-grandfather's secrets, his discoveries and his wisdom.

'Great-grandfather Anso,' he murmured. 'Who would have thought?'

'It does seem a remarkable coincidence that our young apprentice was the one to find Anso's book,' the Captain mused. 'But on saying that, it's a small world when you've sailed to every corner of it.' He shrugged.

Whisker knew the Captain was right. There was no denying the strange coincidences they had experienced on their adventure, but one thing still puzzled him: why?

'Hermit,' he asked, 'where *did* you find the Forgotten Map?'

The Hermit twitched his ears as if awakening a memory.

'Long ago,' he began, 'Hermit visited Captain's Inn on Sea Shanty Island. Old rat came in at midnight, miserable as mud. Hermit offered him friendly drink, yes, yes. Old rat spoke of powerful map in his possession – afraid it would fall into wicked paws.'

The Hermit lowered his voice to a whisper. 'Old rat asked Hermit to keep map secret and safe. Hermit hid map on *Princess Pie* and never saw old rat again, no, no. Map was forgotten. Years later, Hermit discovered map in drawer and went in search of treasure …'

'So the old rat was Whisker's great-grandfather,' Horace surmised.

'And the story explains why the map was known as the

Forgotten Map,' Mr Tribble added.

The Hermit nodded.

'I think it would be best if we continued in this secretive tradition,' the Captain said thoughtfully. 'Who knows what evil creatures will come after the book if they learn of its existence? I suggest we don't speak of the origins of this book again.'

'Aye, Captain,' murmured the crew.

'Very well,' the Captain said. 'It would also be wise if we locked the chest to give the impression that the treasure is still here, should the Cat Fish come looking for it.'

'And we could put something in the chest,' Horace chimed in. 'Something small. Just in case they get the lid open.'

'*You're* something small,' Pete said dryly.

While the crew bickered about *who* or *what* would best fit in the chest, Whisker walked to a dark corner of the cavern and gently placed the glow worm on a rock.

'Thanks for your help,' he said fondly. 'You really brightened things up!'

The glow worm glowed contentedly and wiggled off to explore his new home.

Whisker turned to see Ruby standing silently behind him. She hadn't said anything since they discovered the book, but it was clear she had something on her mind.

'Are you alright?' she asked.

'Yeah,' Whisker said, 'I'm great.'

'He's not,' Ruby said.

'Who? The glow worm?'

'No,' Ruby said, pointing to the small mouse crouching beside the chest. 'Eaton. He'll cop it big time when all the excitement dies down. No one likes a traitor.' She lowered her voice. 'Why do you think he did it?'

Whisker shrugged. 'He'll have a reason. We all have our reasons.'

'Why don't you talk to him?' Ruby said.

'Me?' Whisker said, a little surprised. 'Why me?'

'Because you know how he feels,' Ruby replied. 'Four weeks ago when we dragged you from the ocean, you were the terrified little boy.'

Whisker knew she was right. Part of him still felt like that. He wandered over and sat down next to Eaton. Eaton didn't look up.

'You like books, don't you, Eaton?' Whisker asked casually.

'Traitor books, you mean,' Eaton sniffed.

'Ok,' Whisker said, playing along. 'Why don't you tell me a good traitor story?'

Eaton looked at him suspiciously. 'What do you mean?'

'Well, firstly,' Whisker said, 'did the traitor believe he was doing good or evil?'

'Good, I guess,' Eaton muttered.

'And what did the villains offer the traitor? Was it gold or jewels, or perhaps something more valuable?'

Eaton stared at the ground. 'They asked him if he had a family. He said he only had a sister. They said he'd never see her again if he didn't do everything they asked ...'

Whisker could see the absolute terror in Eaton's eyes, but continued his questions.

'And what happened when the traitor was discovered?'

Eaton struggled for an answer. 'The-the traitor got what he deserved and was locked up or fed to a giant eel or something ...'

Whisker sighed. 'I haven't read that story, Eaton. I only

know the one about the brave little mouse who did all he could to save his sister … that story has a very different ending.'

Tears welled in Eaton's eyes.

'W-what kind of ending?' he asked.

'I don't know,' Whisker said softly. 'It's still being written. But I'm sure it's a good one. It's set on an island of second chances.'

Eaton wiped his eyes with the back of his paw.

'It's going to be a *happy* ending,' he said, looking directly at Whisker, '… for all of us.'

Whisker smiled, the sun moved behind a cloud, the writing on the book faded, Pete placed an old lantern in the treasure chest and Fred locked the lid.

It was time to go.

The Pie Rats left the cavern through the hole in the roof and made their way down the windy slopes. The Captain carried the Book of Knowledge. Fred carried Rat Bait.

'I heard what you did up there,' the Captain said quietly to Whisker as they neared the secret cove. 'It's quite a feat to outsmart Sabre and a brown bear on your own. You've passed your fourth apprenticeship test of *Self-Reliance,* paws down!'

'Um, thank you, Captain,' Whisker said, feeling a tad guilty about the glow worm's assistance.

'I also heard of Rat Bait's feats on the mountain,' the Captain continued. 'He's possibly the only rat more reckless than you, Whisker.' The Captain chuckled to himself. 'I'm glad I was wrong about him. I have a sneaking suspicion we're going to need his help on our next big challenge.'

'Which is?' Whisker asked.

'Winning the Pirate Cup,' the Captain whispered. 'But don't tell the rest of the crew just yet. We have a few islands to search first, and I'd hate for Horace to overexcite himself before the tournament has even begun.'

'I thought you didn't want to enter,' Whisker said in a hushed voice.

'Between you and me, we could use the prize money,' the Captain replied. 'Besides, who can resist the centenary games?'

He stuck his paw in his coat pocket and pulled out a small slip of paper.

'Our official entry receipt,' he said, handing it to Whisker. 'Paid in full by Madam Pearl. She wanted to tell you earlier, but things got a little hectic around here.'

ENTRY RECEIPT FOR THE 25TH PIRATE CUP

The: *Pie Rats* are hereby registered as official competitors for the centenary games. Events to commence on the first day of Autumn, Dagger Island.

PAID IN FULL

Whisker looked over his shoulder at Madam Pearl. She gave him an elegant smile.

'Do you think we have a chance of winning?' Whisker asked the Captain.

The Captain tapped the book. 'Maybe, if our training

regime includes reading ...'

One by one, the Pie Rats scrambled down the rope and onto the deck of the *Apple Pie*.

'All paws on deck!' the Captain commanded, even though the entire crew was assembled in front of him. 'We sail westwards at once.'

'Aye, aye, Captain,' cheered the crew joyously.

The anchor was raised and the *Apple Pie* slowly drifted from the sheltered cove, towing the small yellow boat behind her. She rounded the cliffs and, with a mighty gust of wind, her sails filled with air.

In no time, the *Apple Pie* was racing along the rocky coastline, slicing through the white-capped waves like they were dollops of whipped cream. Whisker felt a new energy surge through his body as he breathed in the salty air. He had escaped the Treacherous Sea, conquered the windy, windy island and was headed for hope-filled horizons.

His enthusiasm was temporarily put on hold when a loud cry echoed down from the rigging.

'Cat Fish ahoy!' Fred bellowed. 'Make haste!'

'Cat Fish!' Pete yelped, almost breaking another lead. 'Where?'

'At the top of the cliff,' Horace cried, rushing to the side of the deck. 'Seven of them!'

'There can't be seven of them!' Pete snapped. 'There are only *six* Cat Fish.'

'There are definitely seven,' Horace insisted. 'Look, there they are, running along. Six little cats followed by one big one.'

'That's not a cat, you blind bandicoot!' Pete shouted, raising a telescope to his eye. 'That's a bear!'

'BEAR?' Rat Bait exclaimed, waking up in the commotion. 'Bear? Where?'

'Calm down, Rat Bait,' Whisker said, rushing over to him. 'The bear's on the island. You're on the *Apple Pie*. We're all perfectly safe.'

'Unless you're a Cat Fish!' Pete sniggered as the seven figures on the cliff disappeared into a clump of pine trees.

'Arrr, me head!' Rat Bait groaned, trying to sit up. 'It feels like I knocked me noggin' on a pile o' rocks.'

'That's not too far from the truth,' Whisker remarked.

Rat Bait glanced around him, trying to fathom what had happened.

'Did ye find the treasure then, Whisker?' he asked. 'What be it?'

'A book,' Whisker replied.

'Oh,' Rat Bait said, somewhat surprised. 'What kind o' book? Adventure? Romance? I be partial to a bit o' romance, ye know.'

He winked at Whisker and then tilted his head in Ruby's direction. Whisker felt his cheeks turning red.

'Non-fiction!' he blurted out. 'It's all non-fiction. It's filled with maps and Rubycies – I-I mean recipes ... and stuff.'

Whisker felt like crawling into a cannon and lighting the fuse. Ruby acted like she hadn't heard him and pretended to tie a knot, with a suppressed smile.

'Aye!' Rat Bait said, clearly impressed. 'The treasure be a book o' some use then!' He reached into his pocket. 'Speaking o' treasure, young Whisker, I still owe ye three pieces of gold for locatin' the chest.'

He pulled out three gold coins and flicked them to Whisker. Whisker caught one with each paw and the third with his tail.

The gold felt surprisingly light to touch, but Whisker knew his limbs had grown strong during his time as an apprentice. He glanced down at the coin in his left paw, expecting to see the banana seal of Aladrya. Instead he saw the unfamiliar design of two paws inside a diamond.

'Freeforian gold,' Rat Bait explained. 'I spent all the Capt'n's gold on retirement real estate!'

'I didn't know Freeforia had a currency,' Whisker said, confused. 'My mother grew up there. Goods were always exchanged by barter.'

'Times are a' changin',' Rat Bait said. 'Rumour has it that Freeforia has a new gold mine. I been hearin' the news from the trader that gave me these coins. Strange fellow he was, a fox with no name, wearin' a long black coat …' He drifted off for a moment, before continuing with his usual enthusiasm.

'I told him I was lookin' to trade me trusty sloop for a smaller boat for me retirement an' he said he had somethin' on offer. The boat be in a pretty bad state, mind you, an' I ummed and arred for some time. He finally threw in a bag 'o Freeforian coins and the deal was done. As a ship repairer, I had no trouble fixin' up the wee vessel, an' look at her now, a golden beauty.'

'So the yellow boat we're towing is yours?' Whisker said.

'Aye, it is,' Rat Bait replied, leading Whisker to the stern of the ship. 'Isn't she something? She has the sturdiest hull I've seen in years – strong enough to survive a cyclone! And look at that carved anchor on the bow. Now that's crafts-rat-ship.'

Rat Bait turned to Whisker for a response. Whisker

stood rooted to the spot, his eyes transfixed on the boat, his paw clutching his anchor pendant.

The boat shone like gold in the afternoon sunshine. But all Whisker could see was red.

'Are ye alright?' Rat Bait asked.

Whisker struggled to find the words.

'Y-your boat,' he gasped in shock. 'I-it belonged to my father ...'

Book 4
The Trophy of Champions

Every four years, the greatest pirate crews on the seven seas gather for an epic tournament of strength and skill.

In the Pirate Cup, there is no silver and no bronze, only gold, gold, gold for the winning team, and the legendary Trophy of Champions.

As an official entrant, Whisker has more on his mind than victory. He is on the trail of a fox in a black trench coat – and an answer …

Discover more about the Pie Rats at:
www.pierats.com.au